LETTING IT RIDE

KATE CAMPFIELD

ISBN (paperback): 978-1-962697-01-9

Cover design by Deranged Doctor Designs

Editing by Melanie Yu (Made Me Blush Books) and Ashley Olivier (Enchanted Author Co)

*For everyone who pined for their big brother's friend,
wishing he'd throw caution to the wind and take you up
against a wall.*

This one's for you.

PROLOGUE

From: Maddox.Anderson@mail.com
To: CamAllen@mail.com
Subject: Re: Fwd: Cruise

That sounds awesome! I'm in for sure. I'm sure Holly won't mind. Open seas, sun, and Bahamas, here we come. Can't wait for a piña colada.
M

From: CamAllen@mail.com
To: Maddox.Anderson@mail.com
Subject: Fwd: Cruise

Just talked to the people about the deal below, and

we're in! You're coming, right? Week of April 14. Four-day cruise to the Bahamas. Details below.

Cam

From: SpecialEvents@RoyalCrownCruiseLines.com
To: CamAllen@mail.com
Subject: Cruise

Let your poker skills take you to the high seas!

Royal Crown Cruise Lines is one of the premier cruise ship travel companies in North America, and we pride ourselves on offering a diverse selection of activities to our guests. For our upcoming cruises to the Bahamas, we are providing guests a chance to gamble with blackjack, poker, and more in our on-board casino. As a special bonus, we plan to offer lessons on poker gameplay and strategy.

As a professional poker player, we can offer you a deeply discounted cruise package in exchange for your expertise in this area.

Interested in hearing all the details? We have plenty of dates to fit your busy schedule! Contact us at the email above or call 800-CRUISES ext. 55 to speak to one of our special events coordinators today. We look forward to sailing with you!

1

CAM

"I'm pregnant. It's, um, not yours." My long-time girlfriend chews on her red-stained lip and shifts her weight from one foot to the other as she tucks her short, dark hair behind her ear. Ellie's gaze moves to the front door, like she's planning her escape from where she's currently standing in the center of my living room rug.

"Are you *fucking* kidding me?" My voice is dangerously soft, but it seems that Ellie is barely listening. It's what I've come to expect: I talk, and she picks and chooses what she hears.

My stomach drops to the floor, the edges of my vision beginning to blacken. Bile rises in my throat as I catch a whiff of her flowery perfume. I used to love that smell.

Ellie and I have been on-again, off-again for almost two years. And yeah, we've been on more breaks than I can count, but when we were together, it was good. Wasn't it? I would have thought that the time we were together meant she owed me... well, something. At the very least, the curtesy to use a goddamn condom when she was fucking someone else.

Fuck. If the baby were mine, I'd do the right thing, obviously. Marry her, raise the kid. Honestly, if she wasn't sure who the father was, I'd offer to do that, too. But if she's certain it's not mine? Shit...

"Cam? Say something." Ellie's blue eyes glisten with tears. It seems almost calculated, but then, maybe I'm just cynical from her manipulating me for the last couple years.

I swallow hard against the lump that rises in my throat, choking off all the terrible things I wish I could say. "Are you sure, Ellie? That it's not mine? You can take a test. If there's any chance it's mine..." I trail off as she shakes her head.

"I know it's not, Cam. And even if there was a chance it was..." Her gaze is cemented to the floor, unable to meet my eyes. I guess I have my answer.

My stomach twists. A wave of nausea passes through me again, and this one has nothing to do with her perfume.

She doesn't say it, but I know.

She doesn't want to have a kid with someone like me, someone with my past. And that tells me everything I need to know. Did we ever even have a chance?

I shake my head in disgust, doing my best to focus on her betrayal, because I can't process the rest of it right now. "What do you want me to say, Ellie? You're having someone else's baby." I wave my hand dismissively.

I wish I had something I could throw against the wall, some outlet for the rage that's boiling up inside me.

She flinches, even though she knows damn well I'd never physically hurt her. Still, it cuts deep all the same. "I just... I don't want this to end badly," she whispers.

I don't even know how to respond to that. *She* doesn't want this to end badly? Then maybe she should have kept her damn legs shut. Or used a condom. Or maybe, she could have just called it quits —again, but for good this time—without sharing all the sordid details. Maybe she should have been honest months ago about her true feelings toward me.

But have I been honest with her? Or myself? Ellie and I were a good match, at least on paper. But was I ever *in love* with her?

I still want to hit some inanimate object, or throw

something against a wall. I want to destroy something, break it apart the way it feels like I'm breaking inside. Maybe that goddamn potted plant that Ellie brought over here a year ago. It keeps trying to die despite everything I've done to keep the stupid thing alive. As I look over to where it sits in the corner, another dead leaf floats to the hardwood floor.

I'm so fucking tired. I was raised to understand that relationships are work. That you have to put effort in to keep things going well. And that's what I've been doing with Ellie, almost since the day we met. Every time we break up and get back together, I remind myself that it just takes work. To not give up.

I've spent so long working on this relationship, and for what? I worked to move on from my past, too, and it gets thrown in my face.

You know what? I'm done with putting effort into things.

I force my fisted hands to relax and let out a long sigh. "I have nothing else to say, Ellie. Congratulations, I guess. Mom-to-be. How exciting." My words sound hollow, even to my own ears, but it's the best I can muster for now.

"I'm sorry, Cam," she says, her voice cracking, the first sign of real emotion she's shown. "We were on a break. And I didn't mean to—"

"Didn't mean to what, Ellie?" I snap. My growing anger has my voice coming out sharper than I mean to, but any chance of peaceful acceptance is now gone. "Fuck another guy? Or get pregnant? Or did you just not mean to do something that meant letting me off your little hook?"

"I..." she trails off, unable to meet my eyes again, and that's when I know that my last line hit a sore spot.

I've been her fallback plan. I'm the one putting in effort to make this work, and I've always been the one she just comes running back to because it's easy. I was never the one she saw a future with.

Maybe not everyone gets a happy ending. Maybe some of us don't deserve one.

"Get out, Ellie." I stalk across the living room to the apartment door and yank it open, my jaw so tight I'm worried I might crack a molar. It would hurt less than Ellie's betrayal, at any rate.

Ellie hesitates, but she finally shuffles toward the door and steps out. She turns and looks up at me. "I really am sorry, Cam," she whispers. "But it was... I tried to get past it, but I..." She gestures at me, as if I didn't already know exactly what she was saying.

She turns away just as I slam the door, shutting her out of my apartment and my life.

I'm so done. With dating, with love, with all of it.

I look over to the corner where that stupid Ficus plant is sitting. Agatha. Yeah, we named the plant. It seemed cute at the time.

But Agatha needs to go. I kick it with my bare foot as I walk by, swearing under my breath when my action just results in more leaves drifting to the floor to join their fallen brethren and a throbbing pain in my foot. I put so much effort into keeping this stupid thing alive for Ellie, trying to prove I could be a responsible plant owner, that I'm a nurturer or some such bullshit.

All that fucking effort wasted, on both Ellie and the plant. And what's the end result? One is dead, and the other may as well be, to me at least. All that effort, everything I did for her, and she can't overlook *one* thing in my past.

I stomp into the kitchen and dig a black garbage bag out from the cabinet under the sink, then stalk back toward Agatha and her rotting leaves.

I kick the couch as I pass, just to take out my frustration on something that won't litter on my floor, wincing at the stabbing pain that results. Now both my feet hurt, and the rest of me doesn't feel any better.

Serves me right.

This plant is leaving my apartment today. I've stressed about keeping this thing alive almost as much as I've stressed about keeping my relationship with Ellie alive.

I take the entire thing and shove it into the garbage bag, or at least I try to, but the stupid plant is too tall. After five minutes of struggle, about eighty percent of the plant is contained in the black plastic, and a smattering of leaves is fanned across the carpet, fallen soldiers in the war against emotions. I grip the top of the garbage bag and haul the entire mess to the front door.

I peek out into the hallway to make sure the coast is clear before I take the bag to the trash chute and shove it down there where there's no chance of getting it back.

Fuck you, Agatha.

2

ADDISON

To: AAnderson@brynmawrschools.com
From: karen_a_morgan@mail.com
Subject: calculus

Hi Miss Anderson,
Thanks for tutoring Rudy with his calculus. It's been a lifesaver. Not sure what we'd do if he got kicked off the high school football team. Since there are no classes over spring break, he obviously can't just stay after school. Can you plan to come to our house to tutor him on those days?
Sincerely,
Karen (Rudy's mom)

To: AAnderson@brynmawrschools.com

From: Judy12044810@mail.com
Subject: Avocados

Don't want to text you during the workday in case you're busy. Can you stop at the grocery store for some avocados on your way home and drop them off here? Your sister and her wife are here and too busy with the twins to go out, and apparently that's all the babies eat. There's green spit-up everywhere.
Mom

"I don't get it." My student scrunches up his face in confusion. He wears this expression so frequently that his face is probably going to end up in a permanent state of bewilderment.

I pinch the bridge of my nose. Calculus is hard, but he's a high school junior who needs to learn this to pass my class. And I can't lose my shit, even if this is the fourth time we've gone over this. Rudy's parents are paying me to tutor him after school, because if Rudy doesn't improve his grades, he risks getting kicked off the football team.

And I need the money, so I can't tell him to simply pack up and get the hell out of my classroom, even if all I want to do right now is take three years off from teaching and drink Mai Tais on a Caribbean island. That would be the life, wouldn't it? No pile of endless responsibilities piling up from everything that I can't bring myself to say no to.

To be fair, even if I didn't need the money, I'd still be here. I can't exactly say no to a student who's struggling.

But for now, I'm choosing to ignore the emails from his mother, because I don't have an excuse to say no. Avoidance is better than direct confrontation. If asked directly, I tend to cave and say yes. I've always been a people pleaser.

There are worse vices, though... Right?

I take a deep breath. "So we're trying to prove this, right? The way we do it is to assume the opposite of what we're trying to prove. Then you solve the problem with that assumption, and you get the answer of zero equals one, which can't happen. Does that make sense? That means our initial assumption must be wrong."

His brows furrow in confusion. "Why?"

Patience, Addie. Just remember how much they're paying you. And plus—and probably more importantly—it's not entirely Rudy's fault. I shouldn't take it out on him. He's been passed along by teachers who were more interested in what the football team needed than what Rudy did. It's not doing the kid any justice.

And it may be selfish, but tutoring on the side is the only thing keeping me afloat. I love teaching, but the salary isn't going to make me a millionaire, and with my schedule, this is the only gig I can really swing right now. And just think: With enough money, that island dream could be a reality. Maybe not for years, but possibly for a few days.

Or at the very least, I might be able to make my rent payment without scraping the bottom of my bank account. Yay me.

Rudy looks at me, still confused, and I try to figure out the best way to explain this to him. "Because one can't equal zero."

"Why?" he asks.

"Because it just... doesn't." How does one even explain this? It should be obvious, especially to a high school junior like Rudy, if his prior teachers had done their jobs.

A football analogy pops into my head. "It's like this. You know how when your team has the ball, they just have one football for the whole team?"

He nods, a spark of something starting to dawn.

"And how many footballs does the other team have while you're in possession?"

"Uhhh... zero?" He blinks, and I think I see the pieces starting to come together.

"That's right. So you can't have one ball and zero balls, right? They're different."

Rudy nods slowly.

I hand him the pencil I'm holding and push the paper toward him. "Why don't you work through this same one, just the way we did together? And then we can tackle another one."

I stand up from the desk to let him puzzle his way through the proof while I dig my phone out of my purse that I keep hidden in my bottom desk drawer. There are about a million emails, all of which I ignore, and one text from my brother, Maddox.

He's busy with wedding planning—I've heard all the details from his fiancée Holly. I can't wait to have her as a sister. I love my older sister, Josie, but she's so much older than me that she's in a different place in her life than I am. She's married and living in Boston with her wife and newborn twins, a world away from my single-and-struggling lifestyle.

My brother is older than me too, so I love having Holly around. She's my age. She's also technically already my stepsister, but that's a whole other story.

MADDOX

> When's your spring break? If it's the week of April 14, any interest in a cheap cruise? Or free. I'm desperate, I'll cover it for you.

> I just accidentally booked nonrefundable plane tickets for our honeymoon and realized I said I'd do this cruise. Please? Holly is going to cut off my balls if I fuck up our honeymoon.

My future sister-in-law threatening my brother's manhood is not an image I want to entertain. Maddox knows I'm almost always willing to help out. It's just who I am, ever since I was a kid.

Maybe it has something to do with being in the foster system before I was adopted, but it might just be how I was wired. I'm a people pleaser. Plus, he had me at *free*. I type out a reply while Rudy continues to scratch his head, my lips twisting in a grimace. Come on, Rudy. You're so close.

> We're on spring break that week. Free cruise sounds sweet. Send me the details, and I'll let you know.

I'm sure there's a catch. There always is, right? But I've never been on a cruise, and I can't exactly afford to pay for a cruise on my own at this point, so this is probably my one chance. I'll look through the information and hopefully there's nothing too crazy. This might be as close to my dream Caribbean vacation as I'm going to get.

I drop my phone into my bag and walk back to where Rudy has written exactly two numbers, neither of them particularly legible. Or maybe they're letters? Honestly, it could go either way. All I know is that whatever he's written is nowhere close to solving this proof.

I tamp down my frustration, more so with myself than with Rudy. I need to do a better job of explaining this. For him, obviously, but I also need this job. Think of how many tacos I could buy with what his parents are paying me for tutoring. Or rent, or groceries. You know, important stuff.

Mom better pay me back for those avocados, now that I think about it. Because even though this thing with Rudy is taking longer than I anticipated, I know I'm going to stop by the grocery store on the way home to do that favor.

I slip into the seat next to him. "Okay, Rudy. Let's go through this again."

Rudy finally manages to show some understanding by the time we're a half-hour past the official end of our session. I breathe a sigh of relief when he heads off to whatever the football team does during the off season. Weight training, maybe?

I love teaching math, and helping kids understand complex math is one of my favorite things. But every job has its drawbacks, and one of the biggest in this job —aside from the meager paycheck—is when students get passed along when they're not ready. Rudy clearly needs some help understanding basic algebra, let alone pre-calculus.

I sit at my desk to finish grading the tests from third period honors calculus. The students in this class are highly motivated and, by and large, highly anxious, so I try my best to hand back tests as soon as possible so they don't lose their minds.

My first year of teaching, I took two weeks to hand back the midterm exams. The number of *Dear Miss Anderson, when will we get our tests back?* emails drove me nearly insane. It also took a ton of time to respond to all of them, which made it take even longer to finish grading the tests.

Now I know better. Grade them the day you give them and ignore as many emails as you possibly can.

I pull out a red pen and go to work, adding corrections and circling errors, although there aren't many. They did well on this one. I tap the pen on the desk, considering whether doing well on a test as a class is a good enough reason for a pizza party or some other reward.

There has to be a better option than pizza. Taco party?

Four tests are graded—fifteen to go—when Annika materializes in my doorway, waltzing in on long legs without knocking. She teaches English on the floor below me, and we've been best friends since we started at this school as brand-new teachers. Her students are terrified of her.

I was too when I first started. She's a straight shooter and loves confrontation—so basically, the exact opposite of me. *No is a complete sentence* is her favorite mantra, especially when the administration starts asking us to use our precious free time to do something else they're not going to pay us for.

"How was the tutoring?" she asks, sliding into one of the student desks. She crosses her legs gracefully at the ankle, the way she once told me princesses are supposed to, her pencil skirt smooth of wrinkles. She pats her blonde chignon, making sure not a single hair is out of place. Her sleek style is a direct contrast to me as much as our personalities. Sometimes I look at her and wonder how we ended up as friends in the first place.

I look back down at my grading as I tuck an unruly strand of my long red hair behind my ear. I've never managed to get anything other than a messy bun to hold my hair in place. "It was good. I'm pretty sure Rudy understands that one and zero are different numbers now."

Annika snorts. "You have the patience of a saint, Addie. I don't even know what I'd do if one of my students was that oblivious. He's lucky to have you."

And she's lucky that the football players all clamor to take their required English classes from Mr. Winston, whose class is apparently boring, but easy. She'd absolutely crucify some of those kids. I caught the tail end of her class once when I popped in at the end of a free block. When none of the students gave what she considered acceptable answers about the underlying themes of King Lear, she added an essay on the topic to their homework on the spot. Five pages.

For the record, I have a college degree, and I still don't know the underlying themes of any of Shakespeare's works. Don't tell Annika.

I circle a red A- on the top of Lily Hutchin's paper and place it face-down in the completed pile. "You make anyone cry today?" I tease.

She pretends to be offended. "I would never make my students cry! I'm warm and fuzzy. I just want them to feel good about themselves even if they can't read." She can't stop a smirk from crossing her face as she tells the lie. "But yes. Only one. I handed back the papers they wrote on A Tale of Two Cities, and there were some real stinkers in there. It's like they don't even try." Her nose crinkles.

"Whose life did you ruin with that grade?" I ask, mildly curious. It's amazing how much the honors students think that one bad grade is going to tank their future. I know I was convinced of this fallacy back in high school, too.

Spoiler: No one cares about your grade in geometry or world history after the tenth grade.

"Joanna Bloom. I just pointed out that if she wrote papers of this caliber in college, she'd get kicked out in the first semester." Annika shrugs.

I bite my cheek to keep from laughing. I happen to know that Joanna just got accepted into the engineering program at MIT. I'm pretty sure she'll be able to get her degree there without ever writing another paper on classic literature.

I circle a B+ on the top of the next paper, cringing slightly. I'm sure this grade will be a devastating blow to David Hannah's honors ego. He and Joanna can commiserate during Chess Club. I add it to the pile before I cap the pen and look up.

"Well, I have news. I might have a lead on something to do for spring break."

Annika noticeably perks up. "Are you reconsidering Myrtle Beach? I wasn't going to go, but I will if you do."

She makes the same salary as me—in other words, not much—but her parents still pay for her to join them on vacations. She invited me to go with them to Myrtle Beach this year, but there's something that doesn't sit right with me about being twenty-seven and bumming a vacation from your friend's parents.

I wave her off. "No, I already told you I can't afford a real vacation, and I don't want to tag along like a third wheel with your family. But my brother texted me earlier. Apparently, he committed to a cruise or something and he can't go, so he's offering me his spot. *And* he's going to pay for it. I'm not sure why he can't just cancel, but I'm willing to check it out."

Annika pulls a dark red lipstick out of her purse and reapplies it, using her phone's camera as a mirror. "That sounds amazing. How many days? Where to?"

Huh. I didn't even think to ask. "Uh... I assume the Caribbean? Are there cruises to other places?"

She lets out a boisterous laugh that echoes off the

classroom walls. I wish her students could see this side of her, the way she is with her friends. Maybe then they'd realize she's actually human. She's strict as shit, sure, but that's because she believes they're all capable of doing better.

Also, I think she secretly likes being known as a hard-ass.

Annika brushes a nonexistent stray hair back into place. "Um, cruises go to about a zillion places. It could be going to Alaska. Might want to check into that before you pack your bikini."

Full house, jacks over tens. A solid hand. I click to raise the bet in the online poker game, then watch as most of the other players fold.

I know Maddox likes to think he's the only good poker player in the family, but I'm not half bad. Although, to be fair, Maddox is the one who taught me everything I know.

One year, when I was about ten and he was seventeen, my parents bought him a poker set for Christmas. He offered to teach me and Josie, and we took him up on it. The buy-in was a king-sized Snickers bar. Santa had put one in each of our stockings, and Maddox wanted all of them for himself.

So, he passed out the chips and taught us the different card combinations and hands. Even back then, he was good at poker, but I had beginner's luck on my side and managed to win the final showdown.

I offered him a bite of one of the Snickers as a consolation prize. That was the last time he wanted to play with me. I wonder if Maddox has started teaching Julio about poker yet. Our mom and stepdad adopted the nine-year-old a year ago, and he's been a great fit for our family since.

From that first poker game, I was hooked and started playing with anyone who was interested. Sometimes for money, sometimes for stuff, but mostly just for fun. I'm pretty good now and make a little extra money playing online poker when I have free time.

The avatars on the screen show their cards, and sure enough, this hand is mine. I click to cash out and leave the game before my luck turns.

There's a new message in my inbox, so I open my mail to see what spam I'm getting now. Amazingly enough, among ten messages trying to sell me things— and thank goodness, none asking me for help with something—one message is a forwarded message from Maddox that starts with *I'll owe you forever*.

I'm pretty sure he owes me forever already, for a variety of reasons, but I scroll down the email chain. He's forwarded me an email from Cam.

Camden Allen.

Seeing the name makes my stomach flip as I picture the sandy brown hair that's always just a little bit messy and the blue eyes that sparkle with gold when he laughs. He's my big brother's best friend and my long-time crush. Like, *long* time.

I've been secretly in love with Cam since the first time I met him, back when I was a gawky thirteen-year-old who hadn't yet hit her growth spurt and he was a cool college dude coming home with Maddox for Thanksgiving. He still lives in Philadelphia, so I see him every now and then, always with Maddox. He's been dating some girl—yeah, I'm jealous—but from my eavesdropping, I'm not sure it's going well.

Is it bad karma if I hope they're on the verge of a breakup?

I know Maddox would probably kill Cam if he ever looked my way. Hell, he might kill me, too. Damn overprotective big brother. Anyway, it's never been a problem, because Cam has never once hinted at any attraction to me. I think he still sees me as that teenager, even though my boobs have finally filled out and I like to think I'm an adult now.

Or maybe Maddox has threatened to gouge his eyes out if he looks at me. I know my brother has threatened other guys with that. It tends to put a damper in my dating life.

There's another email with even more details. Four days, Miami to Nassau. I do a quick online search to find that's in the Bahamas. Nothing seems like a deal-breaker so far. Meals and activities are included, and I'd just have to work in the casino in the evenings for the three nights. Maddox added a line in there that they need one pro and a dealer, so Cam must be going, too.

Excitement flutters in my stomach. From the email, it sounds like I'd just have to deal cards while Cam teaches.

It's a sweet gig, and I'm in no position to turn down something like this. And getting to spend time with Cam is the cherry on top. Who knows? With some one-on-one time, maybe I can finally convince him to give us a shot.

I wrap my hair around my finger as I pull out my phone and check the calendar, even though I know there's nothing else planned. I send Maddox a text before I can change my mind.

MADDOX

> I'm in. Do I need to get plane tickets?

Thank you so much, Addie, you're a lifesaver. Holly says thank you, too. She didn't want to go on our honeymoon alone. I appreciate your willingness to go on a cruise so I can keep my balls.

Um, anytime?

I have plane tickets, but I'll change them to your name and cover the cost of the flight. You get there Saturday morning, and the ship leaves that afternoon. Don't forget your passport.

Can't wait!

3

CAM

A knock on the door startles me from where I'm lying on the couch, a bowl of chips balanced precariously on my chest. I ignore it, hoping whoever it is will go away. It comes again, firm and insistent this time, and I groan as I force myself to sit up. A few crumpled napkins fall to the floor as I stand and set the bowl on the coffee table.

I make a halfhearted attempt to wipe away the crumbs on my shirt as I walk across the apartment. I'm guessing whoever would actually knock on the door to my apartment won't actually care. There are only a few people who are on the list that can come up without the doorman calling.

I open the door to find Miller's disapproving glare waiting on the other side. His gaze roams over my unshaved face and slides down, pausing at the Doritos dust that I missed. Some of the orange powder is still stuck to the same t-shirt I've been wearing for three days.

I follow his gaze. There might be some Cheez-it remnants there, too. I should add more of those to my grocery delivery.

"Dude. You look like shit." He steps past me into my apartment, not waiting for an invitation. He has a bag slung over his shoulder. I consider asking if he brought snacks, but the look on his face tells me he's not here to play around.

I close the door behind him, scratching the hair on my jawline. I usually shave daily, but I've let it go for a while since Ellie, and it's getting pretty thick. And itchy, come to think of it. I wonder how Maddox keeps up with his beard year-round. It seems like a pain.

I survey the living room as I follow Miller, wincing as I see it from his point of view. This place really is a shithole. Maybe I have let things go a little.

He doesn't say anything as he picks up the snack bowl from the coffee table along with two empty soda cans and heads for the kitchen.

"Hey! I was eating those," I protest. They were almost gone, but still. Don't take a man's chips.

Miller ignores me. He comes back empty-handed a

few minutes later. "We'll deal with cleaning in a minute. It's time for you to rejoin the living. Go take a shower."

"I've showered," I lie, trying to sniff my armpit without him noticing. Do I not smell or am I just used to the odor?

He scoffs. "Yeah, I don't believe you. Go shower now and I'll see what I can do to air out the smell of body odor in here. It smells like a teenage boy's room." Miller's jaw is set.

When he gets an idea in his head, there's no changing it. We've played poker together for a few years and aside from Maddox, he's one of my best friends. He loves to play the class clown, always trying to get people to fall for his latest pranks, but when shit hits the fan, he faces things head-on. I've always loved how perceptive he is and his way of dealing with things with bluntness and brutal honesty.

I mean, I usually love that about him. Especially when it's aimed at someone else. Not so much right now. Because I'm fine. I showered... maybe four days ago? I sniff again. The point is, I'm good.

Miller holds up two more soda cans and a pair of black socks that I vaguely remember taking off a week or so ago when I realized there was a hole in the toe of one of them. "Go, asshole. You stink."

I'm not in the mood to argue. I'm not in the mood for much of anything lately, to be honest. I've broken up with Ellie more times than I can count, but this last one wrecked me. I'm playing like shit, losing money left and right to the point where I'm on the verge of losing sponsors and having to get a real job. Just one more thing in my life that Ellie can ruin.

I wish I drank. This seems like a situation where a few beers would really help. Or a whole bottle of gin.

I shuffle over to the bathroom and reluctantly turn on the shower. The hot water does feel good, as does the filth sluicing off my body, but fuck if I'll admit that to any of the guys.

Since Maddox met Holly, he and I haven't spent as much time together. He knows about the thing with Ellie, of course, but he was so busy with wedding planning that I didn't get to go into all the details with him. I just told the two lovebirds that Ellie and I broke up and that was why I wasn't in a great mood.

I believe Holly's instructions were *Pull your shit together for one day or I'll rip off your nuts*, but I'm paraphrasing here.

With Maddox wrapped up in love, I've gotten closer to Miller and Blake, the other member of our informal poker club, although Maddox is still my best friend, at least on paper. I'll take any friends I can get these days, though.

I feel better as I step out of the shower, smelling like Irish Spring instead of stale cheese dust. But I'm not really sure I want to feel better. A large part of me just wants to keep wallowing in my misery. I'm done trying.

But in attempt to get Miller off my back, or at least out of my apartment so I can return to doing nothing, I shave the scruff that's turned into a full beard and put on deodorant. I draw the line at hair gel. I only use it to perfect the messy hairstyle—yes, the messy look is intentional—and as I'm not planning to leave this apartment anytime soon, the baseline mess is fine.

The guy looking back at me from the mirror when I'm finished at least looks like a guy who didn't recently have his heart ripped out. I think that was the goal, but it doesn't make me feel better about my situation.

I emerge from the bedroom wearing a clean t-shirt and a pair of sweatpants, because let's not go too crazy here. I'm willing to put on a shirt and pants if I have to, but like I said, I'm not leaving the apartment. Everything I need is right here, courtesy of several different food delivery apps and streaming video apps.

The living room has transformed in the twenty

minutes since Miller sent me to take a shower. The empty cans and used plates have disappeared from where they had accumulated next to the couch. There's a vague scent in the air, something I'm not used to. It's like... fruity and summery or something. I sniff again.

"It's a scented candle," Miller says, walking out of the kitchen. He's folding a towel that I didn't even know I owned.

Sure enough, there's a pink candle flickering on a side table next to the TV. "Who uses scented candles? And where did that come from?"

Miller rolls his eyes, like I'm the one asking stupid questions. "Anyone who doesn't want their house to smell like ass, you moron. My mom sends them to me all the time. That's why my place smells good. I brought you one, along with some carrots, because I'm guessing you've eaten nothing but processed shit covered in artificial cheese dust for the last few weeks. I'll tell her you just said thank you."

I wonder what it would be like to have a mom like Miller's. Or Maddox's. The kind that are all in your business, but in a sweet, helpful way. "Well, thanks for cleaning up. But I'm fine."

Miller crosses his arms over his University of Scranton t-shirt, blond hair falling in his face. The man always looks like he needs a haircut, yet somehow, he's the one here lecturing me on cleaning myself up. Go figure.

"Cam, you know I love you. But we're worried about you. All of us are. Maddox has been drowning in wedding stuff and honeymoon plans and Blake is at some university thing or they'd be here, too. Ever since you and Ellie broke up, you've been in a funk," he says, a crease forming between his brows.

"I have not." I totally have. It pisses me off to have it pointed out, though.

He points at me. "You've pulled out of two tournaments. You've skipped almost all of our games. Between Maddox getting married and you throwing your little pity party, it's been just me and Blake half the time, so we end up not even playing. And are you even playing online anymore?" Miller's eyebrow arches. I hate that he's right.

I let out a long, dramatic sigh. "Fine. I'll snap out of it. If I have to."

Miller gives me an approving nod. "Besides, I think you just need to find a rebound. We all know Ellie did a number on you. We've been by your side for this whole messed-up relationship, and I'll admit that the way it ended was particularly brutal. But you have to get back out there, man."

I'm about to argue, but maybe he's right. Maybe I need to remind myself that there are other girls out there. I mean, I'm not going to fall in love. Or even get in an actual relationship, because you can't trust anyone but your friends these days. That ship has sailed.

And I still believe what my parents taught me, that you have to put in work to make a relationship last, and I'm not in a spot to put that work in for something long-term. But I could see myself going on a date or two. Maybe even having some sex. It's just been me and my right hand for a little too long.

Miller sits on my couch, wiping away the last of the crumbs from the coffee table with a grimace. "Let's get you on a dating app."

I frown. A shower was one thing. Dating apps are another. I pull my gaze from where it's fixed on the coffee table to give Miller a side-eye. "Fuck no, man. I'm not doing that."

He gives me a withering look. "Why the fuck not? We've all done it. Those girls are single, or at least they're supposed to be. They're generally not pregnant with other men's children." He raises a brow. "The bar is low here, man. You can go out with a few of them."

I flop down on the couch next to him. "I guess. I'm not against going out with someone, trying to move on. I'm just not great company right now, and I'm not ready for an actual relationship."

Miller opens his mouth and then closes it again, like he wants to say something but is holding back. He changes the subject. "Are you still doing that spring break cruise thing?"

The cruise. I perk up. I'd almost forgotten. Maybe we're all past college and our real spring break days, but that's what I need right now, more than a girl from a dating app. A chance to leave reality and my life behind for a little while.

"Yeah. I'm leaving in..." I pull out my phone to check the dates. There are a bunch of texts on there that I haven't bothered to open. I swipe past them to open my calendar. "Less than a week."

Miller nods, satisfied, as he picks up a dead leaf from underneath the couch. I knew I missed a few when I was dragging Agatha out of the apartment. "Good. Use that as a reset. Find a girl to fuck, or at least to spend time with. It's a limited time engagement. You'll both be there for a few days, so there's no pressure. Just something to help you move on."

I nod. This idea is growing on me.

"And Cam?" Miller looks pointedly at me. "Don't forget to shower."

4

ADDISON

To: AAnderson@brynmawrschools.com
From: PSmith@brynmawrschools.com
Subject: Senior class advisor

Hi Ms. Anderson,

I've been informed that Mrs. Niedermyer has stepped down as the senior class advisor. Of course, this is a critical time with prom, graduation, and the like coming up quickly. Could you step in for her? Thanks so much for your help.

Patricia Smith

Vice Principal, Bryn Mawr High School

To: AAnderson@brynmawrschools.com
From: RudyFootballGodXX@mail.com
Subject: math

Hi Miss A,
I'm taking the SATs in a couple weeks. Is there math
on there?
Rudy

T he bell rings, a blessed sound that signifies
the end of the school day. The students, of
course, have been busy packing up their
bags for the last ten minutes, despite my still standing
at the front of the room lecturing.

I can't blame them. Friday before spring break?
There's not much I can teach right now that's going to
stick. They're all ready for a week of vacation and
putting school out of their minds, and for the first
time since I started teaching, so am I.

I wave as they file out of my classroom, thinking
through what I need to get done. I'm mostly packed,
but I need to add a few things in the morning, like a
toothbrush and such. The airport is only about thirty
minutes from my place, so I'll take a rideshare to the

airport for my flight. I calculate backward from the time my flight leaves. Half an hour to get to the airport, fifteen minutes through security, fifteen-minute buffer… an hour should do it.

Annika is coming over for our weekly pizza and movie night, so she'll lock up the apartment after she leaves.

I shimmy a little. Time to party.

Or whatever one does on a cruise.

It occurs to me that I should have looked into this more than twenty-four hours before I'm supposed to leave. The email said we'd get a shirt of some type to wear while we're working, but beyond that, I have no idea.

Was I supposed to pack formal wear? Running shoes? Hiking boots? I know we're stopping in Nassau, but what exactly do we do there?

"Spring break!" Annika sings out from my doorway.

I grin at her. "How do you always get up here so quickly? Do you leave the classroom at the same time as your students?" I tease.

"Sometimes before." She walks in with a shrug, her Coach tote slung over one shoulder. "What movie are we watching tonight?"

I check my purse to make sure I still have my

phone and car keys. "I was thinking something old school. Arsenic and Old Lace or something. But I need to pick your mind about cruise stuff. You've been on one before, right?"

She nods as we walk together into the hallway. "Wow. It feels like a ghost town today," she says, looking behind us.

We're the only ones in the hallway. The click of Annika's stiletto heels echoes off the cinder block walls. Usually, students would still be all over the place a few minutes after the bell, but there's no sports practice or after-school activities the day before spring break. Seems like the students couldn't get out of here fast enough. But can you blame them?

Annika and I turn the corner to head down the stairs toward the first floor as she keeps talking. "Anyway, yes. I went on a few cruises when I was little with my parents. I'm sure they've changed since then, but I can give you the gist. And we can look it up online. Did you pack already?" she asks.

"I figure it's warm, so I packed shorts and the bikinis I bought when we were at the King of Prussia mall a couple weeks ago." Really tiny ones, cause why not? "And I packed some workout clothes in case there's a gym, as well as a couple of sundresses. It's only a four-day cruise, but I don't know if I need to be fancy or be ready for outdoorsy stuff or what."

Annika pushes open the heavy door that leads to the back parking lot. "That should be perfect. I remember there being some fancy restaurants on the ones we went on, but we just didn't go to dinner there. There are usually a bunch of options, so just go where you're comfortable." She pauses and looks at me. "Are you sure you're okay going alone?"

I thought I told her the whole thing, but maybe I left out a few details, like the ones I've been obsessing over in my head. "Oh. Right. I'm not going alone, actually. Remember my brother Maddox?"

"Yeah. Of course. Is he going?" She wrinkles her nose, thinking. "Didn't he just get married?"

"Yes. No. I mean, no, he's not going, because yes, he just got married. He and his wife Holly are leaving on their honeymoon tonight. But he signed up for this cruise deal a while ago with his friend and didn't realize the dates overlapped when he booked the honeymoon. And lo and behold, you get married, your spouse wins when it comes to them versus friends. It was a deal they got where they needed two poker players, so I'm standing in for Maddox."

We reach Annika's car first. She pulls open the

driver's door of the Buick sedan and tosses her bag on the passenger seat. "So, who's going with you, then?"

I shift my purse back up on my shoulder. "He was supposed to go with his best friend, Cam. So now I'm going with Cam." I bite my lip.

Annika narrows her eyes at me. "The one you had a crush on when you were younger?" Of course she'd remember that tiny detail I'd failed to mention.

"Yeah." And maybe I might still like him a little bit now, too. Oh, who am I kidding? If anything, my crush has only intensified over the years.

"He still hot?" She slides into the car.

Hotter. "I guess." I shrug.

She pulls her sunglasses from the compartment near the rearview mirror and slides them on. "I want to see pictures. I'll see you at your place in an hour."

I paw through my duffel bag, double checking that I have everything I think I need. Cutoff jean shorts, check. Sundresses, check. Two itty-bitty bikinis that look damn good on me, check. Hair product, hair dryer, makeup, face cream for daytime, face cream for nighttime, sunscreen—check, check, check.

I can't help but think about Cam while I pack.

Every time I put something in the duffel, I'm subconsciously—or perhaps consciously—wondering if Cam will like it. What he'll think when he sees me in an outfit, or what he'll think of my eyeliner.

It's been like this for years. Any time I know I'm going to see Cam, I overthink my decisions, consider how he'll take something. But in the last ten-plus years, it hasn't made any difference. I'm pretty sure I could prance in front of him naked and he wouldn't even notice.

I'll be pretty close to naked in these bikinis, so I guess we'll find out.

A few butterflies flurry in my stomach just thinking about it. Maybe he'll see me in one of these outfits and he won't be able to help himself. All the flirting I've tried to do for years will finally be worth it as he steps closer to me, runs his hand up my—

The buzzer announces Annika's arrival and brings my daydream to a screeching halt. I toss everything back in the duffel and zip it up before I buzz her in. A few minutes later she's at the door, pizza in hand.

"Did you get pineapple on it this time?" I ask, closing the door behind her.

"Of course." She rolls her eyes. "I forgot one time, okay? I always get pineapple on your half."

She tosses the box on my kitchen counter and

sweeps her white-blonde hair into a messy bun while I flip the box open, our Friday night ritual down to a science. I take a slice from the half that has pineapple, leaving the pepperoni and green pepper—*ew*—for Annika. We settle on the couch in front of the TV, balancing the plates on our knees.

She brings her slice to her mouth while I reach between the couch cushions to find the remote. "So, do you have pictures of Cam?" she says through a mouthful of sauce and cheese.

One of the things I both love and hate about Annika is that she cuts right to the chase. "Yeah. Hang on." I come up with the remote and hand it to her along with my plate while I hop back up to grab my phone.

I scroll through the pictures until I find one from Maddox's wedding day and hand the phone to Annika. "Here. He's the tall one next to Maddox. Light brown hair."

She takes the phone from my hand, studying it with a nod. "I'd call that dark blond, but yeah. And blue eyes? Hot as fuck, especially in a tux. Are you sure you don't still have a crush on him? Because if he's not spoken for, feel free to give him my number."

I snatch the phone back with a glare. "I'm not giving him your number."

Annika smiles triumphantly as she bites into her slice of pizza. "A-ha. So you do still like him. No wonder you're so excited for this cruise. You get to look at your brother's best friend shirtless for a week."

"Four days," I correct. "And he's not interested in me like that. Plus, how do you know he'll be shirtless?" Not that I'd complain about that view. I lift my own slice to my mouth and blow on it before taking a bite.

"All the pools and such. But," Annika says through a mouth full of pizza. She swallows and dabs at her lips with a napkin. "I've seen you in a bikini, girl. How could he not be interested? And he's going on this cruise with just you. That's something, right? He doesn't hate you, at least."

Cam definitely doesn't hate me. He's always been nice. Brotherly, which is even worse.

You can fuck someone you hate. You can't fuck your brother or someone who sees themselves in that way. It does surprise me a little that Cam wasn't upset about Maddox pulling out of the cruise at the last minute.

Wait.

I swallow my bite as a flash of panic rises in me. "Uh, I think he knows I'm going. Crap. I'd better check."

Annika just raises her eyebrows and shoves more

pizza in her mouth as I wipe my greasy fingers on a napkin and text Maddox.

MADDOX

> Hey, you told Cam you pulled out of the cruise and are sending me instead, right?

> Maddox?

> Uh, you told him, right?

Oh, fuck.

My phone lights up with a call from my brother as Annika raises the remote and starts to scroll through movies. I leave my plate on the couch as I stand and walk into my bedroom.

"Maddox? Please tell me you told him. I don't want to fuck up your honeymoon, but please. Tell me he knows that the whole plan changed."

I close the door to drown out the noise from the TV as credits from an old movie start up. My duffel bag is waiting on the floor by the closet, packed full of those tiny shorts and bikinis and ready to go. Crap, I hope I'm not springing this on Cam.

"Hey, Addie. Nothing's wrong. It's just..." I can

hear the wince in his voice. "I was so busy planning the wedding, and then the honeymoon, that I just... forgot."

"Forgot what?" I twirl a finger in my long hair, pulling slightly. It's a nervous habit, but one that I don't plan to give up anytime soon. I finally stopped chewing my nails when I was in college. Let me have this one.

Maddox married his wife Holly a month ago, and they're leaving on their honeymoon to Italy tonight. I only texted him because I know he's at the airport, so I'm not *technically* interrupting their honeymoon yet. Their flight leaves in half an hour.

"I, uhh..." He pauses when a mumbled voice in the background announces something about someone being welcome to board. "Fuck, I have to go. They're boarding our flight. Anyway. I completely forgot to let Cam know I had to back out and that you were going instead. It'll be fine, though. Cam is cool, and he'll be there if you need anything. He'll take care of you. Have fun, okay? I'll try to send him a quick text right now."

He disconnects the call, and I stare at the phone in my hand. God, I hope Cam isn't pissed.

But you know what? That's future Addie's problem. For now, I take a deep breath, leave my phone on my bed, and settle back on the couch with pineapple pizza, my BFF, and a classic tale of two old ladies and their little murder habit.

Everything will be fine.

I'm probably forgetting something.

I toss my toothbrush, toothpaste, and deodorant into the duffel bag, trying to remember if there's anything else I didn't pack. I throw in an extra pair of flip flops and zip the top. I need to get moving, so whatever's packed is packed at this point. No time to stress over it now. I like to cut it close when it comes to flying. The less down time in the airport, the better. Why should I spend my time being bored there when I can just get there when I need to?

Annika is still snoring on my couch as I tiptoe through the apartment. With how often she and I stay over at one another's places—almost every Friday night, after a couple of hard ciders—we should really just find a two-bedroom and move in together. But she says we're adults and that twenty-seven-year-olds shouldn't have roommates, and she's not wrong.

I trust her to lock up when she leaves later on. Annika is a much more functional adult than I am. She remembers to change the oil in her car, pays bills on time, and has matching mugs in her kitchen. When the light on her hallway ceiling burned out, she found a ladder and replaced it.

I just used alternate lighting sources for three months until Maddox came over and replaced the bulb. He's tall enough to reach it without a ladder.

Part of me understands why Cam still sees me as a kid. The rest of my family does, too. It's probably things like the lightbulb. I'm sure Maddox has told all his friends the stories about me, like the time I drove to Vermont and back for a friend's wedding and didn't realize I'd need to fill up with gas to make it all the way back. He was the one I called, trying to figure out why my car had just stopped and why I was stranded on the Garden State Parkway.

But this week I can be whoever I want to be. A *mature* woman. Someone who knows how to change lightbulbs and fill a gas tank and say no to people asking me to sacrifice my time and energy to do things like take over planning prom.

I close the apartment door behind me and head over to the elevator. We're officially on spring break now.

5

CAM

I can do this, right?

I stare at the small dark screen for a few more seconds.

People lived for hundreds of years without phones at all, and then for decades without smartphones. I can leave my phone in the car. I don't need it on the airplane, and I can live without it while I'm on this cruise.

It'll also make sure I don't get any messages from She Who Shall Not Be Named.

I check my messages again to make sure I haven't missed anything. What if there were an emergency? Then, surely, I'd need a phone.

I've been looking forward to this cruise for months. Ever since I came across this opportunity in the first place, even before we got accepted, my plan has been to leave my phone behind. I was going to let everyone know I was going off-grid for a few days so they wouldn't freak out if I didn't answer a text, and then just live in the moment.

The living in the moment thing was only part of the goal, to be honest. I'm also not sure about international data plans and roaming fees and what-not. So it's also a bit financially motivated. I make good money with poker, even with my recent bad run, but you never know when your luck is going to run out.

Now that the moment's here, though, I'm not so sure I want to live in it.

What if someone needs to reach me, someone who doesn't know I'm leaving my phone behind?

Or what if I need to... check social media?

Okay, not a good reason, since I don't even have accounts on any of the platforms. But I could, if I wanted to. And maybe I don't have any good reason to hang onto my phone. But for safety, I decide I'm going to compromise. Bring it along, but turn it off.

My thumb holds down the button to turn the phone all the way off before I toss it into my duffel bag. It can stay there until we reach the shore on the way back.

My plane takes off for Miami in two hours, which gives me plenty of time to get from the parking garage to the terminal and pass through security with enough time to relax without feeling stressed. I'm leaving tonight and staying in a hotel, so I don't have to rush to make it to the ship tomorrow.

I'm not sure when Maddox is getting here, but he's an adult and can figure out things on his own. He's probably flying in tomorrow morning, cutting it close as usual. He's been so busy with his wedding to Holly that I haven't wanted to bother him.

Goddamn people in love.

He's missing out, if you ask me. He's dealing with making sure Holly is happy and cleaning up after the dog they adopted, while I'm people watching and browsing through the airport bookstore in search of something to read on my three-hour flight. Maybe not the most exciting stuff, but I'm happy. And not stressed about making my flight.

I settle on a murder mystery just as an overhead speaker announces that they're starting to board my flight.

I settle on the bed in my hotel room, shirtless, with the box of food and the TV remote in my hand. Unwilling to eat in a restaurant alone, I ended up ordering a pizza that I had delivered to the hotel. It's familiar and comfortable after the weeks of wallowing in misery.

Eating delivery while shirtless, that is. It's been so long since I've watched cable TV that I almost don't remember what's on each channel. I've eaten two slices of pizza—extra sauce, extra cheese, and pineapple—before I settle on a movie on the Hallmark channel.

My mom loves Hallmark movies, and I grew up watching them with her. I'm pretty sure she wanted a daughter, but after three boys, she gave up trying and just did the girl things with the three of us.

For example: Have you ever had a pedicure? It's a magical experience. Every man should try it at least once. I tried to take Maddox with me to get one shortly after we graduated from college and were trying to figure out our lives. He told me, in no uncertain terms, that pedicures are not an appropriate bonding experience for bros.

He's the one missing out, if you ask me. I wiggle my bare toes. I'm an adult now, which means I can go get a pedicure whenever I want—and I did, just in time for this cruise. There's not a callous in sight.

I grab another slice out of the box and take a bite as

the main characters are torn apart by a miscommunication that could have been avoided if they'd only talk to one another like adults.

Maybe when I'm ready for another relationship, I should look for a girl who's a talker. The more you talk, the less likely you are to miscommunicate, right? I let out a snort of laughter as I think of Addison, Maddox's sister. She's a talker. I'd bet any guy she dates knows exactly where she stands. I can picture her laying it all out there during one of her epic tirades.

I shake my head with a grunt. Why does the idea of Addie dating someone bother me? It shouldn't matter to me one way or another if Addie's in a relationship, other than making sure the guy she's with treats her like a princess.

She's a sweet girl and deserves the world. Just off-limits for me. It's always been that way.

It made sense when I met her—she was thirteen and I was twenty and in college, and I'm not a perv. But then she grew up, and... I noticed, okay?

It's hard not to notice Addie Anderson. She fills up a room with her smile. But like I said, she's off-limits. Maddox has made it clear that he doesn't want any of his friends going after Addie, and my friends are my life. I can't risk ruining the friendship I have with him.

I push any thoughts of Addie out of my head with a defeated sigh.

By the time the main characters have figured out that they're in love and are living happily ever after, I've eaten half of the pizza, which is probably too much, but I don't care. I summon the energy to get up and throw away the leftovers before I tuck into bed for the night.

I'm so used to having my phone that I feel naked without it. It takes me a few minutes to realize I can just turn on the light and read the book I bought at the airport.

It's been less than twelve hours since I turned off my phone and already I'm going through withdrawal.

The story draws me in as soon as I open the book. There's something about the solid feel of a paperback, the smell of new pages. I settle in, planning to read just one chapter. But is it ever really just one?

I sleep in as late as I can while still having time to shower before the hotel's checkout time. One chapter last night was definitely not enough. It was almost 1 a.m. before I finally convinced myself to put the book down and turn off the light. Now I remember why I don't read before bed.

I force myself out of bed and into the shower, stopping at the coffee maker on the way. The cruise leaves in the afternoon but starts boarding passengers around noon, and as usual, I like to get places early.

I check in and board the ship, the warm air brushing my face as my boss for the week, a fit thirty-something woman named Harper who introduces herself as one of the event coordinators leads me along one of the decks shows me to my room. Her blonde ponytail swishes behind her as she points out the movie theater, the casino, two different bars and a restaurant.

"There are four decks of guest rooms above us, then the pools and gym and all of that are on the higher decks. Your room is down this way."

Harper leads me down a set of stairs and through a long hallway, finally pausing beside a door.

"This is it," she says, opening the door to a very small room. "You have a closet there"—she gestures—"and there's a bathroom with a shower through that door. Fairly simple, but of course you have access to everything on the ship when you're not working, so enjoy. There's lots to do."

This room is about the size of a postage stamp, but

we got a good deal on this cruise, so I'm not complaining. It's not like I'm going to spend much time in here anyway. I checked out the cruise line's website, and there seem to be endless options for things to do once we leave port.

Harper hands me a pamphlet, if you can call it that. It looks more like a short novel.

"There are maps of each deck in there, so you can use that to find things on the ship. Like I said, you're welcome to take advantage of anything we offer. Anything at all."

Did she just bat her eyelashes at me? Maybe there's hope for a rebound this week after all. She's cute, I realize. About my age, probably. Tanned, fit... I could do worse.

I flip through the pages as she keeps talking. The ship is massive, even more than I realized from our walk through one deck. Multiple restaurants. Several pools, a playground, mini golf and other games. Pickleball, whatever the hell that is.

I bookmark the page that shows the pools and the gym, as well as the running track.

"Your uniform shirts are in the closet. You'll need to be wearing them when you work, but otherwise, you don't need to identify yourself as an employee, since you're really not. When you're off-duty, you're off. You'll be working the evening shifts." Harper hands me a paper. "This is your schedule. There's a laundry room down the hall that you can use. Meal schedules and all of that are in the handbook. Questions?" She clasps her hands in front of her.

My brows furrow. I'm still trying to figure out where my room is located on the maps in this book.

"We're here," she says, answering my unasked question. She puts a hand on my arm as she flips two pages and points to a tiny square in the middle of a hundred other identical squares.

Ah. There it is.

I can see myself getting very lost this week. I make a mental note to leave in plenty of time and to carry one of these maps with me. Of course, knowing Maddox, he probably figured out how to download these maps from somewhere on the internet and has been studying for the last couple of weeks.

I haven't talked to him since his wedding a month ago, which is strange for the two of us. We used to live in the same building and hang out multiple times a week. But I guess that's what happens when you get married, right?

You stop having time for your other friends.

"Good luck!" Harper chirps, pulling the door

open. "Have a great time. Look forward to seeing more of you soon."

She flashes me a wink before turning away. The door shuts behind her, and I look around the small room. There's not much in here, which makes sense given the size of the space. A small sofa, a desk, and a set of bunk beds.

Judging from the size, it looks like a standard twin bed, which means my feet will hang off the end, but I guess beggars can't be choosers.

I toss my duffel on the bottom bunk. The early bird gets the worm, so Maddox will have to deal with the top bunk. I turn around to explore the rest of the room. One door opens into a closet, with room to hang clothes and a few shelves. There are a few uniforms hanging on the rack. I shut the door and open the other one, which is just slightly larger and opens into the tiniest bathroom I've ever seen.

There's not much to take in. A toilet, an itty-bitty corner shower that looks like I'll have to duck to get my head under the spray, and a sink that's barely large enough to wash my hands. But again, not complaining. *Free* trip. And I promised Miller I'd shower while I was looking for my rebound, so I will. Just in a very... small shower.

I go back to the bed—it takes eight steps, I counted

—and open my duffel bag. I may as well put some things away, since I don't have much to do until about eight o'clock tonight, when we're working in the casino. Maybe dinner, I guess, if Maddox ever gets here.

I put a couple bathing suits on the shelf and hang a few t-shirts on the remaining hangers. My fingers brush against my phone at the bottom of my bag, but I resist the temptation to look.

I'm trying to figure out where in the world to put my toothbrush—yeah, the sink is that small—when I hear Harper's voice again, and the door to my quarters opens.

I push open the bathroom door, wondering whether Maddox is finally here or if Harper just forgot something. I step out just in time for a sweep of red hair and a smattering of freckles to hit me like a gut punch.

Long pale legs stretch down from cut-off denim shorts that are so short I can almost see the curve of her ass. A cropped tee barely contains a pair of tits I know I shouldn't be staring at, but I can't look away from them. Caramel-brown eyes meet my gaze, and I feel myself start to melt in their heat before I pull myself back and try to figure out what the hell is going on.

What the fuck is Addie Anderson doing here?

6

ADDISON

To: AAnderson@brynmawrschools.com
From: PSmith@brynmawrschools.com
Subject: Re: Senior class advisor

Hi Ms. Anderson,

Have you given more thought to being senior class advisor? It's just a few months, until the end of the school year. If you're okay with it, can you finalize a list of prom themes and ideas for graduation celebrations over this week off and have them sent to me on Monday when we return?

Patricia Smith

Vice Principal, Bryn Mawr High School

To: AAnderson@brynmawrschools.com
From: Judy12044810@mail.com
Subject: (no subject)

Addie,

Have a great time on your cruise! When are you going to be back? Josie and Chris are in town with the kids, house sitting and dog sitting while Maddox and Holly are away on their honeymoon! Remember all the avocados they went through last time they were here? Now Julio is getting obsessed with avocado toast. I've created a monster.

Mom

Cam pulls a hand through his sandy brown hair as his gaze rakes down my body. A rush of heat goes through me, wondering if he's finally *seeing* me. But when he meets my gaze, his brows are furrowed in confusion and his blue eyes flash with... anger?

Fuck. He's not just confused. He's pissed off, too. Shit. This combination of emotions points to one very obvious conclusion.

He had no idea I was coming.

And now I'm furious, as well. Maddox said he was going to text him. He had *one* fucking job.

It's not hard at all to see it from Cam's perspective, and I can't help but be mad on his behalf. Picture this scenario: Cam books this vacation planning on spending some time with his best friend. Then said friend bails, and not only does he *not* tell Cam, but he sends me, his little sister, in his place.

I'm going to kill Maddox. But from Cam's expression, I might have to wait my turn.

"Okay, have fun! Cam can fill you in. He has all the details. See you guys soon!" the too-cheerful event coordinator chirps from behind me, completely oblivious to the tension that fills the room.

She shuts the door behind her. It latches with a thud, and the air in the small room suddenly thickens even further, making it hard to breathe.

Cam's poker face is abysmal right now. Unlike my brother, he rarely uses it outside of games, so I can read every emotion that flits across, and none of them gives the sense that he's happy to see me.

A pit settles in my stomach while I give him a minute to recover, but he looks like he's locked into some sort of internal debate.

I clear my throat. One of us has to break the silence.

"Um. Hi, Cam." I heft my duffel bag higher on my shoulder. Putting it down seems like accepting the inevitability that we have to share a room, but it's getting heavy. All those little scraps of fabric add up.

Cam blinks as he comes back to reality. "Uh. Hi, uh, Addie. What, uh..."

I can tell he's trying to find a nice way to ask what the fuck I'm doing there. I force out a laugh, trying to go for the isn't-this-funny, we'll-laugh-about-this-later vibe. "So, uh, it looks like Maddox didn't text you."

His brows knit together even further. There's no trace of humor in his expression. "Text me about what?"

Okay, I don't want to have to be the one to spell it all out here. It makes me look like I had something to do with this, or like I planned it somehow. All I did was offer to help my brother.

A light finally comes on, his eyes growing wide with something that looks suspiciously like horror as realization dawns. "Wait, are you here instead of Maddox?"

Ding ding ding.

I give up on the duffel and let it slide to the ground. "Yeah. He accidentally double-booked this and his honeymoon, so he asked if I could take his place. I can't believe he didn't let you know. He said he was going to text you when I talked to him last night."

"Well, he didn't." Cam pushes his hand through his hair. The movement leaves patches sticking straight up, like they're alarmed at the situation, too. Shaking his head, he blows out a breath. "But I also turned off my phone yesterday. I was going to do like a detox, stay off the grid for the next few days. I might have turned it off before he texted."

So maybe Maddox did text, but it was clearly at the last minute. This is on him, obviously. Restitution will have to be paid.

I start to think through ways to get him back for this. What about that blue dye? The one you stick in someone's food without them knowing and it makes them piss blue? I've used that one on friends before. They freak out, especially guys who absolutely lose their shit if something seems to be threatening their manhood. Seems like a fitting punishment in this case. I bet Holly would help me.

Cam runs a hand over his jaw. At least he's unclenched it. "Shit, I'm sorry, Addie. I didn't mean to freak you out. I'm just surprised, is all. I was kind of expecting a boy's trip and to reset after some shit in my life."

There's the Cam I know, the one who would

rather walk through fire than hurt someone he cares about. He doesn't hold grudges the way I do. Maybe I won't tell him about my plans for revenge against my brother. I get the sense Cam would try to talk me out of it.

I pull on the piece of hair that's wrapped around my finger, then loop the hair around again. "It's okay. I think I'd react the same way. And I'm kind of surprised too, if it helps. Maddox didn't mention that we'd have to share a room. I..." What did Cam say? Some shit is going on in his life? Suddenly, I don't care as much about sharing a tiny room or who's on this cruise. "Wait, what's been going on in your life? Is everything okay? Want to talk about it?"

Cam's eyes widen once again. You'd think he'd be used to my rambling by now. He's certainly been around me enough to know that once I start, it's hard to turn off. But when he turns his head to the bunk beds behind him, I realize it's not that. It's that he hadn't processed the sharing a room thing yet.

He looks to the other door, the one he was standing in when I showed up, then back to me. "Yeah. It's not exactly a ton of space."

That might be putting it mildly. It's not lost on me that he's ignoring my other questions about his life. I suppose that's fair. We don't really have that kind of relationship, at least not yet. I decide not to push it. If he doesn't want to talk about it, that's his business.

"I don't take up a lot of space." I shrug a casual shoulder.

Cam just nods. He looks deep in thought. About the room or the cruise or whatever is going on in his life?

"So, can I, um..." I gesture around the room with my hand. "Is there somewhere I can put my stuff?"

"Oh. Yeah." Cam pushes his hair back again—his favorite move—and pulls open a door I hadn't seen. It's a shallow cabinet, already half full. There are two shirts hanging from a bar, and stacks of t-shirts and shorts on the shelves. Cam reaches in. "I also didn't realize we'd be sharing. Let me just..."

He moves his clothes to one side to open up a little space. I unzip my duffel and put a few pairs of shorts on one shelf, shirts on another. I pause. Do I unpack my bikinis while he's standing in front of me? What about underwear?

I'm hoping to use the time we have together to convince him that I'm all grown up, that I'm a viable dating prospect and that maybe, just maybe, we belong together.

He's certainly known me long enough that he should know whether or not he could like me that way.

But I'm not sure displaying my purple thong five minutes after he realized he's stuck with me is going to be the most effective strategy.

I decide to leave the rest in my duffel. Underwear and swim suits don't need to worry about wrinkles, so they'll be fine stored there. The bag of my toiletries takes up a good amount of space as well, but there should be room in the bathroom for that. I pull it out before I zip up the duffel and kick it to the side of the room.

"Is that the bathroom?" I angle my head toward the one remaining door, my toiletries container in one hand. The hairdryer and flat iron are still in the duffel, but I don't need them until at least tomorrow. I managed to fit almost everything else into this container.

Cam nods. "Yeah. It's pretty small, though."

I pull the door open and somehow manage to keep my jaw from dropping. *Pretty small* is an understatement. It's a closet. It's actually smaller than Annika's walk-in closet. This is where I'm supposed to change my clothes?

Clearly, the designers of these rooms didn't factor super awkward roommate situations into their planning.

There's a sink, but no counter. Where do you keep

the flat iron and hair dryer and hair products? Not to mention makeup. Maybe I can try for more of a natural look this week, like beachy waves or whatever.

Who am I kidding? My hair doesn't do natural. It needs to be tortured into submission. If I don't have my products, we're looking at messy buns for the whole vacation.

Cam moves to stand behind me in the doorway. My body registers his heat immediately. "I guess maybe you could put the case on the ground?"

I nod silently. Where to store things isn't really my concern. On the floor is just as good as anyplace else. It's more that I like to spread out while I get ready. It's not like I can hold a hairbrush, flat iron, and texture spray in my hands all at the same time. Something needs a place to sit.

With a resigned sigh, I put the case on the floor beneath the sink. I'll sort this out later. There's no point to freaking out about the space issue because one, there's nothing we can do to change it, and two, because it makes me look high maintenance.

And maybe I am when it comes to this. We all have our vices. I just don't want all of mine on display for Cam all at once.

I consider the space again. Maybe I can put the makeup on the back of the toilet or something.

Cam takes a step back when I turn around. "So, uh, Harper left me a guidebook thing. It has maps in it and information about stuff. Let me give it to you so you can look through it."

I've never heard Cam sound so unsure. He's more laid back than Maddox or some of his other friends, but he's always projected this air of quiet confidence. It's one of the things I always liked about him. It's such a contrast to my personality, where I fill any possible space with talking. If I'm happy, I talk. If I'm upset, I talk. If I'm nervous, it's like word vomit, and I can't stop it.

I feel bad that my being here is screwing with his plans, whatever those were, and that there's something going on in his life that he needs to escape from for a while. But at the same time, this is probably the one cruise I'm going to get to go on in my life, and I'm going to take full advantage of everything here.

Cam hands me a bound stack of papers that's so thick it feels like a textbook. I peer glumly around the small cabin, then settle on the sofa, which is surprisingly uncomfortable. I twist, trying to get situated, but it makes no difference.

With a huff, I flip open the book to the first page, then look up.

"Sit. Let's look through this together," I offer,

scooting further to one side and patting the rocklike surface next to me.

He wordlessly lowers himself to the couch.

This is so awkward. I've known Cam forever, and it's never been like this. Usually, conversation flows easily. We tease one another, banter back and forth. But we've never been one-on-one. There's always Maddox and usually the rest of my family to provide a buffer.

I'm feeling pretty out of my element, too. My go-to icebreaker of saying something funny or silly has to go on the back burner, even though jokes are all that are popping into my head at the moment. I know Cam thinks of me as a little kid. Maddox's baby sister. That's all I've ever been to him.

And this week is about being whoever I want to be, and right now I feel like being a mature, confident woman.

Not mature like old. Just... mature. Not the baby of the family who has to be the Christmas Elf delivering presents to all the family members from under the tree because I did it once when I was three and it's never gone away.

Every freaking Christmas. *Addie, be the elf and hand out the presents!*

It's cute when you're a kid. As a twenty-something, it seems like they're just having fun at my expense. The last few years, I've had to force a smile while doing my present elf duties, trying to hold back the outpouring of emotion that tends to spill out when I've tried too hard to keep things bottled up inside.

I hold the guidebook between us so Cam and I can both see the pages. "So, it looks like this ship is huge. Where are we on these maps? Might be easier to start from there."

Cam slides a little closer to me. His arm brushes mine as he reaches over to flip a page in the book, and a spark of electricity shoots through me as my breath catches, reminding me of those years I've pined after him.

I hate that Cam sees me as just Maddox's little sister. Do older siblings ever realize their little brothers and sisters have grown up? Or are we younger siblings always locked into the "baby of the family" position?

This is my chance to break out of the mold. Maybe not for my family, but for me. And Cam, who kind of counts as family. At least, he sees me the same way they do.

Until now. I can be a mature woman.

"...There." Cam points to something on a page.

Dammit. A mature woman would be paying attention to what he was saying. I can't admit I zoned out already. Pretty sure that if I said, *Can you repeat that? I was busy thinking about licking your abs and being the Christmas Elf,* it would not move our relationship forward.

He'd probably find the phone he hid away somewhere and call Maddox to come pick me up like a kid getting in trouble at school, honeymoon be damned.

I settle for noncommittal. "Mmm, "I say. "What else?"

Cam turns a page—another arm brush, another tingle—and starts to tell me about the pools on the upper deck while I do my best to keep my body from spontaneously combusting from being so close to him.

It's hot in here, isn't it? And humid. I mean, of course it is. It's mid-April and we're in Miami. The weather here is obviously going to be different from what I left behind in Philadelphia.

I rub a sweaty palm on my shorts and turn the page in the guidebook. As we've flipped through the pages, I've done my best to focus, and I think that now I have the tiniest bit of a handle on where things are around here. At the very least, it's not like I can leave the ship. I'll find my way back to our room eventually, even if I get lost.

Being this close to Cam is getting a little intense, at

least from where I'm sitting. Cam, however, seems totally unfazed. I search for a reason to distance myself, just a little bit.

"Do you mind if I change?" I ask him, pushing the guidebook onto his lap. "It's pretty warm in here. I need to change my shirt." We'll blame it on the weather, even though almost anyone would argue that you can't get much more warm-weather-appropriate than a crop top.

But it *is* hot in here. It's just not the weather, entirely. It's mostly the man next to me.

Cam takes the book from me and turns another page, seeming oblivious to my internal struggles. "Nah, that's fine."

I pull open the closet and take the first tank top off the pile I put in there a few minutes ago, then hold it up. This one is more modest than some of the others I brought, so a good choice for now.

I turn in a circle while I look around. This room is small. Did I mention that? Like, really small. And right now, it feels even smaller, because I don't want to pull my shirt off in front of Cam.

Right. Bathroom. That'll work.

"I'm, uh, going to change in the bathroom," I say, cringing at my own words. Did I really need to *announce* it like that? Dear lord. This whole being a mature woman is not going well.

Cam finally meets my eyes, and I can tell this is the first time that this part of things has crossed his mind. That we're stuck together, and part of sharing a room is changing clothes near one another. I mentally cross my fingers that he won't think this is incredibly awkward.

But as I watch, his pupils dilate as his gaze lowers to my chest before he snaps it back to my face.

It's not much, but it gives me hope. That once we get past the weirdness of this situation and he stops seeing me as Maddox's little sister, there might be a chance for us.

In the distance, a horn blows, signifying that the ship has left port.

And that we're trapped together.

7

CAM

The afternoon has been... interesting, to say the least. I like Addie, I do. She's always been fun when I hang out with Maddox's family, which is a common occurrence, especially around the holidays.

We have a long history of being friendly and even teasing one another. This cruise should be just as much fun as those gatherings.

But every time I've seen Addie in the past, it's with the buffer of her family and, most importantly, her brother. Because sometime in the last several years, I realized that Addie wasn't the kid sister I met all those years ago.

She's grown up. And she's absolutely gorgeous.

And way, *way* off limits.

It hasn't been a problem, because Thanksgiving dinners don't exactly lend themselves to one-on-one conversations or even flirting. But since she showed up here, it's just been the two of us.

Thank God Addie suggested getting out of our room and exploring the ship. The cabin seemed small when I first saw it, but once Addison walked in? It shrank down to next to nothing.

I'm a good guy, or at least I like to think I am. But fuck if this cruise isn't already testing me.

Four days, Allen. Keep it in your pants.

"Let it ride," the player across from me says, leaving his bet in place on the green felt of the poker table without raising the bet.

I drag my attention back to the poker game I'm dealing, focusing on the game in front of me and trying to block out the noise of the hundreds of people jammed into the casino. The lights are low, but the excitement of night one of the cruise is palpable among the passengers.

I give the player a nod of acknowledgement and look to the next, who folds. This first night of the cruise, I'm mainly just dealing cards, with a little bit of how-to advice thrown in there. Tomorrow, I'm supposed to give more strategy advice and teach people not only how to play but also how to play well, something I used to think I knew how to do.

If they saw my recent track record, they might not want their lessons from me. Since Ellie fucked me over, I've been on the worst losing streak of my life. I'm lucky that my history with this game gave me enough of a buffer to ride out the losses.

But tomorrow night, for better or worse, Addie and I will work together, with her dealing the cards while I sit at the table with the other players, explaining strategy and playing open hands. For tonight's shift we're both dealing, each at our own table.

I'm doing my best to concentrate on the game, but it's tough. Not the dealing cards part; that I could do in my sleep.

What's tough is keeping my eyes off Addie.

I started out the evening checking on her from time to time—just looking over to make sure she was comfortable, that she knew what she was doing. All innocent stuff, of course.

I never knew Maddox's little sister knew how to play poker, let alone deal, so I figured she might need some tips.

Turns out she doesn't need my help at all.

She's a natural, that red hair swirling around her as she deftly hands out cards with a broad smile. People are flocking to her table, and I'll admit I'd do the same if I had the option.

She has this way about her that's almost electric. I've never seen Addie outside family settings before, or maybe I've never noticed this side of her. She's an entirely different person. With her family, she takes on the role of the youngest sibling—happy, putting others at ease but never taking control.

But here she's confident, outgoing, with a laugh that puts a smile on the face of everyone around her. It's almost the opposite of the Addie I thought I knew, but she actually seems more... herself, somehow. It's like her confidence is hers alone, rather than her just being what her family expects.

She's stunning.

Addie turns her head just slightly and our eyes meet, and everything around us fades into the background.

It's like we're in an old movie, where everything is black and white, but we're the only ones in color. Addie's smile stays in place as she tilts her head. She's too far away for me to see the flecks of gold that I know dance in her eyes when she's happy, but I know they're there.

"So, what happens after we place our bets?" a

woman at my table asks, pulling my attention back to my players.

Jesus, get a grip, Cam. Addie may seem different when she's away from her family, but she's still Maddox's little sister. We're not in a fucking movie. If we are, it's Dead Man Walking.

I give the woman a dazzling smile, hoping she'll forgive me for ignoring her.

"Now, I deal out three cards. These are called the flop." I turn them over one at a time as the four people seated around the table watch earnestly. "Then we bet again, and I turn over a fourth card, then a fifth with betting each round. You have your two cards in your hand, too. For this game, you can choose any five cards to make your best hand."

The player next to me frowns. "Do we have to use the ones in our hands?"

"Not for this game. We're playing Texas Hold 'em. But other poker games, the rules can differ. For tonight I'll just teach you the rules you need for this game."

Nods all around.

I coach the players through placing their bets for this round, and only one folds. It's easy to stay in when you're playing for fun rather than betting your own money.

Out of my peripheral vision, I'm still watching

Addie's table. An older gentleman—good-looking, sure, but gray-haired—gives her a wink when she turns over the fifth community card.

I grimace. Back off, sir. She's way too young for you.

She's too young for me, too, I have to remind myself. Even if I were interested. Which I'm not. Because it's Addie.

Keeping an eye on her this week is going to be tough. I owe Maddox that much, and even though he *did* kind of leave me high and dry by sending Addie in his place, he's still my best friend. Making sure his baby sister stays safe and out of trouble is the least I can do.

But it's only been half a day, and the more I look at her, the more trouble I have reminding myself why she's not an option.

I turn over another community card. I'm kind of doing this on autopilot at this point and looking forward to when I can actually teach strategy, because the strategy these players are using is mostly to just toss in their bets and then to leave them there without folding or backing off, even when it looks like the hand is a loser.

But again, it's their money. And tonight, it's not even their money. They got a stack of free chips at the door to use however they want. They run out, they can get more.

"How are you hanging in there?" Harper materializes behind me. She's shed the white collared shirt that identified her as a crew member earlier in the day and is now wearing a low-cut little black dress that wraps around her athletic body, emphasizing a tiny waist and narrow hips.

Between her blonde hair and the rockin' body she's displaying, she should be exactly my type, but I'm just not feeling it. Maybe it's just that I've been in a funk since Ellie. I should try to give Harper a chance.

"Pretty good," I reply, my gaze moving back to the cards as players place their bets on the last round. The ones who are still in the game lay down the cards in their hands and I push the pile of chips toward a couple that's been playing together. "Full house wins."

They stack their chips gleefully while I gather the cards and shuffle them.

"Want to get a drink?" Harper asks, grazing a hand over my shoulder. "You can take a break. There are enough tables available."

As I've cleared the cards, most of the players have vacated my table anyway. It can't hurt to talk to Harper. Maybe I just need to get to know her a little. Miller told me I need to move on, after all.

I look at the one couple remaining, the ones who won the last round. "Are you guys okay if I step away for a bit?"

They nod and cheerfully gather their chips before heading to Addie's table. The woman gives me a little wave as she turns away.

"Come on. I'll get you a drink," Harper beams, heading for the bar.

I run a hand over my jaw. Harper's an attractive woman. She is. And the expression on her face makes it obvious that she's interested in me, if the wink she gave me earlier today wasn't enough.

What's the worst that could happen? I said I was looking for a rebound, right? Plus, she works on a cruise ship that sails from Miami. There's an expiration date for anything that would happen here, so I don't need to worry about any messy fallout or emotional entanglement.

I give her a slow smile. "That sounds great. I'll take a soda."

Harper tosses her honey-blonde hair over one toned shoulder as she hands me a glass.

I sniff and take a sip. The bartender offered to

make me a mocktail, something with soda water and orange juice and something else. It's decent enough.

I thank Harper and bring the glass to my lips again. "So, how long have you worked on the ship?"

She gives me a smile that seems practiced and sips at her own drink, some concoction that appeared to be mainly alcohol with a splash of pineapple juice. "A couple of years. It's a fun job, and I get to travel. Like, what's not to love? Spending every day on a ship like this?" She lets out a tinkling laugh. "I'm sure at some point I'll come back home to put down roots, but this is a blast for now."

"Where's home for you?" I'm not sure this is information I need to know about my rebound, if that's even what she's going to be. Her interest in me seemed to wane slightly when I told the bartender to make me something non-alcoholic.

"Southern California. San Diego." She tosses her hair again.

"That seems like it would suit you." I set my glass on the high-top table between us.

Harper dabs at the corner of her mouth with a bar napkin. "It does, one hundred percent. I'm a total California girl. Blonde, tan, loving the sunshine, the whole thing. How about you?"

"I'm from Philadelphia." I don't have much to

elaborate on here. I lift my gaze above Harper's head to see how Addison is doing. She's still at her poker table, dealing cards and looking completely relaxed and content. The smile stretched across her face is genuine.

No wonder the players are flocking to her. I feel a sudden urge to leave Harper here and be closer to Addie.

"What are you planning to do tomorrow? Any big plans for our day at sea?" Harper's question pulls my attention back. I need to pull it together. I can't keep getting distracted by Addison. But then again, that's part of my job this week, right? Keep an eye on Addie. Keep her safe. Even if I didn't read Maddox's text, I'm sure that's what it says.

I pick up my drink and shrug. "No idea, really. Hoping to just relax. Maybe I'll hit the gym or the pool. What about you? Do you work all day, every day?"

She wrinkles her nose and shrugs, taking another sip of her drink. "I'm working most days while on the ship. I get a day off when we dock in Nassau. Maybe I can show you around while we're there. I get to explore at least once a week."

I wonder how often she *explores* with a new man at her side. I get the sense that Harper does this often— choose a passenger and flirt with them for the duration of the cruise. I'd guess it's frequent. She has a practiced air about her flirting. It's effective, don't get me wrong. It's just very clear that she's done this before.

Across the room, Addison clears her table and piles chips neatly in a case before she rises from the table. She's still chatting with two men who are sitting at her table, even though they're no longer playing, and suddenly, I'm uncomfortable.

"Would you excuse me, Harper?" I ask, draining the last of my drink.

She swallows more of her cocktail and nods, a small smile on her face. "Of course. I'd love to have a chance to hang out more this week. I'll look for you tomorrow."

"Sounds good." I give her a nod as I place the glass on the table between us. I haven't worked through the logistics of having a rebound fling on a cruise ship, I realize, even if I want to, which is still a big *if.* It's an absolute shitshow inside my brain right now as I try to process emotions around Harper, Ellie and Addie.

I need to be rational, logical. Put Ellie out of my head for good. And then consider all the angles and pick the one who checks all the boxes. It should be easy, right?

Messy emotions aside, there's no way I can bring a girl back to the cabin I'm sharing with Addison even if

I wanted to. I don't think having sex while Addie's on the top bunk would count as "looking out for Maddox's sister."

"Addie, let's head back," I say as I near her table.

The two men who are still talking to her—flirting, I can tell now that I'm closer—pause and look over their shoulders at me. They both look too old for her, too experienced, too—well, everything. She needs to stay away from guys like that.

Addie raises an eyebrow at me and turns her charm back to the men. "Would you excuse me, boys? I'll be here tomorrow night. Look forward to talking with you then." She beams.

I'd really rather she not talk to them at all, but there's no need to make a scene. I wait to move until she rounds the table to stand next to me. We walk together out of the makeshift casino—it's some other kind of activity space during the daytime, apparently— and along the dock.

"How was your evening dealing cards?" Addie asks. She glances over her shoulder at the men we just left before looking up at me.

I blow out a breath. "It was good. Kind of boring,

but fun. Did you have fun?"

That smile stretches across her face again. God, she's gorgeous. "I did. It was so much fun. I've never really dealt cards other than in family games, so I loved it. Everyone was so friendly."

Looking at Addie, that beaming smile across her gorgeous face and her collared shirt unbuttoned just enough to give a hint of cleavage, I can see why everyone was so friendly. I realize I'm looking down Addie's shirt and jerk my gaze upward to Heaven, to atone for my sins or something.

Off limits.

"You and Harper seem to be getting along," she says cautiously.

There's a hint of something in her voice, a tone I can't quite read. "Yeah. She seems cool." That's about all I can say about Harper so far.

"The guys at my table tonight seemed really nice, too. Maybe I'll see them again tomorrow." Addie winds a strand of her long hair around her finger.

I shake my head. Over my dead body. "Addie, be careful. You don't know who these guys are. It's fine to be friendly and all while you're dealing cards, but don't get roped into other things. I don't know what you were expecting this week, but Maddox will have my ass if you do something dumb and I don't look out for you. You have to be safe."

"But you can hook up with our boss?" There's a hint of jealousy in her voice.

I sigh and pull on the back of my neck. *Shit.* This is not going well. "Addie, I'm not hooking up with her. She asked me to get a drink. And it's none of your business."

She whirls on me, fire flashing in her eyes. "That's literally the same thing I was doing, Cam. I met a couple guys. They wanted to flirt. Maybe I did, too. Who cares? End of story. And I'll echo right back to you: It's none of *your* business. So stay the fuck out of it."

She yanks open the door to our cabin and stalks inside.

Shit. She has a point, but I need to shut this down. "Don't say the F word," I retort as she slams the bathroom door.

Don't say the F word? Where the fuck did I come up with that? She's not a third grader.

She opens the door and pokes her head out. "How the fuck old do you think I am, Cam? I'm a fucking adult. I'll say fuck whenever the fuck I fucking feel like it. And fuck whoever I fucking want to." She slams it again, and I hear the *click* of the lock engaging.

I wince. She has a point, but I don't want a fight, especially not tonight, and I've been around Addison enough to know when Hurricane Addie is about to blow through. Definitely not something I want to deal with tonight. It's the coward's way out, but I'm going to lay low and let the storm pass over.

I'm not ready to admit that it's not just her temper I'm avoiding.

I climb into my bottom bunk and turn the light off, then close my eyes. For now, Addie is safe and sound in our cabin, and I don't need to worry about the guys she was talking to. It's not that I don't want her dating or anything. That's really not my business. She can hook up with whoever she wants.

I just want to keep her safe. That's all.

But if I'm honest, it's not that. I don't like the thought of her with any man. And that's exactly what I'm not ready to think about.

And I know if we keep having this conversation, I'll not only think it; there's a damn good chance I'll say it, and that's not fair to Addie. She doesn't need to know how fucked-up my thoughts are right now.

When the bathroom door pushes open, I concentrate on slowing my breathing.

"Cam?" Addie whispers. Her voice is husky, and the sound goes straight to my dick.

I don't respond. I pray that she can't see the clench of my jaw in the dark.

The bed moves slightly as she climbs onto the top bunk and tosses herself back and forth, getting comfortable for the night. I wait until she stops moving and her breathing evens out before I slip out of my bed and head into the bathroom to brush my teeth.

I stare at myself in the mirror. It's so small that I can barely see my whole head at once. "What the fuck are you doing, Cam?" I whisper to my reflection.

I've always thought Addie was cute, liked to tease her. I maybe even had a little crush on her at one point. But it's never gone beyond that. Besides my loyalty to Maddox, I've never let myself think of her as more.

I spit the foam out after brushing and grip the sides of the sink. Addie is off limits. Don't even think about her like that.

Just don't.

8

ADDISON

To: AAnderson@brynmawrschools.com
From: ANickerson@brynmawrschools.com
Subject: plants

Addie-
Did you forget about your plants? I've been watering them. You're welcome. You can pay me back in pizza when you're back. How's your crush? You have Wi-Fi there, right? Send me a text. I need to hear the play-by-play!
Annika

I stretch in the bed, my arms reaching out as far as they can without hitting the wall. I peek down to realize my nipples are beaded into stiff points that are easily visible beneath the sheer tank top I wore to bed, and I jerk the covers up to hide them before I realize it's silent in here.

I pick my head up from the pillow and look around. "Cam?" I call quietly. Maybe he's still asleep.

I kind of hope he is, actually. I realized last night that I didn't have any pajamas. I knew I was forgetting something. Maybe I should have focused on exactly what I was putting in my duffel bag instead of daydreaming about Cam.

Anyway, it seems like those daydreams are just going to remain fantasies for now.

After I came out of the bathroom, Cam seemed like he was asleep. I was kind of relieved that I didn't have to fight with him. I have a fiery temper, one I like to attribute to the redhead in me, and I can usually carry an argument on long enough to win. But buried beneath the relief of avoiding confrontation, I was almost... disappointed.

I thought maybe, just *maybe*, we were getting somewhere with having a conversation. Like maybe there was a chance he was seeing me as an adult that he could actually talk to.

I don't really know why. It's not like he's shown much interest in me other than pulling me away from the guys at the poker table, and that seemed more big-brother-y than the protective urges of a guy who's into you. Most of his attention last night seemed to go to Harper.

I sigh and stretch again. I wasn't sure last night if he was fast asleep or if he was going to wake up if I made too much noise, so I did my best to shimmy into a tank top and out of my clothes under my covers, just in case. As much as I want him to see me as a dating prospect, I don't think the first thing he wants to see in the morning is my barely-covered ass, especially before he has his coffee.

I hold onto the railing and peer down at the bottom bunk.

No Cam. The sheets are pulled up and nicely tucked in. He made his bed on a cruise ship? I have questions. About the made bed as well as the fact that Mr. Night Owl was up before me.

I climb down the ladder, leaving my sheets messy, and try the bathroom door. It swings open, but no Cam. Huh.

I look around for some clue as to where he's gone and finally spy a note on the couch.

ADDIE—
WENT TO GRAB A SMOOTHIE AND THEN TO WORK OUT. PLANNING TO BE AT THE POOL LATER IF YOU WANT TO MEET ME THERE.
—CAM

He woke up and left the cabin to work out? That reeks of him avoiding me. I've never known him to voluntarily do anything before 10 a.m.

But now that I think of it, getting a workout in seems like a good idea. I need to burn off some of this frustration. And I need to figure out exactly what my game plan is here. My original plan of *show up and show some skin* doesn't seem to be working so far. It's been less than twenty-four hours, but we're on a tight schedule here.

It also slowly dawns on me that I didn't actually have much of a plan beyond the skimpy outfits. What am I going to do if he calls me out on it? If he realizes I'm into him and tells me he's not interested?

I don't want to picture that scenario. And I need a

Plan B, clearly. My favorite way to clear my mind and really think is to work out, so that's where we'll start. I brush my teeth and hair as best I can without getting claustrophobic in the small bathroom, then pull on a pair of spandex shorts and a sports bra for the gym. I wrangle my mass of hair into a messy bun and secure it with two hair ties.

I'll give Cam the benefit of the doubt, I decide. Maybe he was tired last night. But he hadn't even brushed his teeth before he climbed into bed. I mean, maybe he was *really* tired. God knows I'd have to be bone-tired to forget to brush.

I frown at myself in the small mirror. Was he just avoiding talking to me, faking sleep until I passed out? I know he hates fighting, a stark contrast to my love of confrontation. I've never understood it. Why wouldn't you just put it all out there and have it out?

Other than telling people you're into them, obviously. That's different.

But on a scale of behaving-at-work Addie to the Hurricane Addie my family knows, last night was on the mild side. My outbursts can get lots worse. But Cam's seen worse, more than once. Last night shouldn't have pushed him over the edge.

I sigh as I tuck my phone into my shorts and grab a pair of earbuds to bring to the gym for some background music while I work out. There's Wi-Fi on the ship, which is a nice surprise.

Okay, maybe it's not a surprise to anyone but me. I kind of thought we'd be drifting out here with no connection to the outside world, like some kind of Bahamas-bound luxury pirate ship. But then again, I also had no idea cruise ships were so... expansive, I guess. This ship is basically a floating Ritz-Carlton. No wonder people pay so much money for these trips.

I scroll through emails while I start on the elliptical, using one hand to hold the handles while I use the other for my phone.

There are eleven emails from work that I try to ignore before I cave and read ten of them and respond to three. Forty-two are spam messages trying to sell me something—*delete*—and one email from Annika. I open that one, which is another quick note telling me to have a great time and to bring her all the dirty details. Nothing about my plants this time.

I wish I had some dirty details to share.

Annika is likely to have some advice, and I think I need another person's perspective here. I open up my texts and send one off.

ANNIKA

Need advice on Cam.

I put the phone on the stand in front of me, then pop my earbuds in and crank up my music, losing myself in some classic 80s rock while I think.

Maybe he's just not interested, but the way his eyes darken when he looks at me tells me there must be something there. Is it the whole best-friend's-sister thing? That seems like the most likely explanation, honestly.

Jesus, I'm a grown adult, and my big brother is still ruining my life the way he did when I was fifteen.

I'm almost done with my cardio when a text pops up.

ANNIKA

The crush? What's going on?

I pause the music as the timer on the elliptical hits thirty minutes, a perfect warmup before I get to the reason I came here in the first place. I wipe at the sweat on my forehead as I climb off the machine, then type out a text as I head toward the weights.

It feels like he's ignoring me. We kind of got into a fight last night, And we're sharing a room, and last night he went to bed without saying goodnight while I was in the bathroom. I don't think he even brushed his teeth.

Ew? Maybe he was tired.

Maybe. Or maybe he was faking sleep. Who knows.

Wait, back up. Sharing a room?

In a very brother-sister kind of way. There are bunk beds.

Hmm but maybe potential for something?

Potential for what? Hooking up in the top bunk? This isn't college.

Fair enough. But are you looking for a hookup? I know he's hot. I saw his picture, but from what you've told me, he's been your brother's best friend forever.

I think I like him. Like, really like him.

I'm feeling braver over text. Yeah, I told Annika I wasn't into him before I left. It was a lie. Obviously.

I knew it! You thought you could hide it.

Okay, yes. I want him. But like, more than a hookup, I think.

> How would your brother feel about all this? Didn't you say he's always told Cam to stay away from you?

> If you want to bust out of your rut and live a little, I support you. But don't do something you're going to regret.

Shit. I slide the phone into the side pocket of my shorts. She's right, and I hate it.

Maddox has always told Cam to stay away from me. *Always.*

I never thought there was a chance for me with Cam, but then I caught him looking at me over Thanksgiving dinner one year when I was something like twenty-two years old.

I'm pretty sure Maddox saw it, too, because ever since then, I've heard Maddox tell Cam I'm off limits more than once. If Cam and I hooked up and Maddox found out, he would kill Cam, then kill me, and then kill us together all over again.

Should I just forget the whole thing? Look for someone else to have a little vacation fling?

The idea of something short-term with a guy I don't know sounds oddly safer than getting Cam to realize I'm interested in him. Because a vacation fling doesn't have to work out. There's no expectation beyond these few days on the ship.

If I let Cam know I'm interested and he doesn't reciprocate, I still have to see him back home and relive the humiliation of putting myself out there. And if he *does* reciprocate, we'll both have to deal with the fallout when we get home.

I nod to myself. A stranger is safer. It'll be fine. I just can't think too much about why the idea fills me with disappointment.

I force myself to pick up a set of small weights and start on my bicep curls. Lifting will keep my mind off of other things. I focus on my form in the mirror. Okay, I'm only half focused on my form. The other half of me is watching the other people in the gym. Specifically, searching for Cam.

He said he was going to work out, and I was hoping he'd be here, but there's no sign of him, which is probably good if I'm trying to push him out of my mind. I know he runs a lot—Maddox once told me he did cross-country in college—so maybe he's running. I think I saw a jogging track listed somewhere on all the maps.

There are plenty of other cute guys here, all with six-pack abs and toned biceps and thighs. All with absolutely no strings and zero ties to my brother, too.

I check my posture, squeezing my shoulder blades together. From what I read in last month's Cosmopolitan, it's healthier for your back. Plus, it has the extra benefit of making your boobs stick out. No complaints there.

I head over to a bench and slide weights onto either side of a barbell for bench presses, then reconsider and pull a couple off the end, not wanting to lift too much without a spotter. The last thing I need is to drop a weight on my neck while we're in the middle of the ocean. That wouldn't do much for my mature, confident woman image.

"Do you want a spot?" a deep voice asks.

I look up to find an attractive man peering down at me. The scruff over his chin reminds me of my brother, which doesn't help the attraction, but it seems to work on him. He's smiling as he makes no move to hide his obvious perusal of my body.

So maybe the boob thrust worked after all.

"Sure." With a spotter, I can lift my usual weight. I slide the five-pound plates back onto either end of the bar and settle onto the bench.

"I'm Grant," he says as I bring the weight down.

"Addison," I grunt out as I push it back up. I'm hoping that was at least a little ladylike, but I doubt it. I lower the weight for another rep.

"You have nice form." Grant's hands hover, ready to take the weight if I need him to.

Biting my lip, I check out his arms. His biceps are huge, and he's got at least four inches on me in height from what I can tell by looking up at him. He's not as tall as Cam, but he's got more muscle.

I manage six bench presses with the heavier weight before I rack the bar. "Want me to spot you, too?" I ask as I sit up.

Grant sizes me up, like he's not sure I can handle the kind of weight he wants to lift. I tense my abs to make the muscles more obvious.

"Sure. Let me swap out the plates." He pulls off the smaller weights that I stacked on either end of the bar and puts another forty-five-pound weight at each side.

I do the math in my head. Ninety pounds per side equals 180, plus the forty-five-pound bar. So, 225 pounds. Not bad.

He adds a ten on either side. I blink.

Okay, 245. I hope he doesn't actually need a spotter. That's heavier than I usually deadlift.

Grant settles on the bench below me, and I stand in the spotter's position while he does his reps, stopping after fifteen to take a break.

"You need more weight?" I ask, hoping he's maxed out, but he's barely broken a sweat.

"Uh..." Grant looks at the weights stacked on the

bar, probably doing the same math in his head. "Yeah. Can you grab me two ten-pound weights?"

I grab them off the floor, shamelessly leaning over to give him—and whoever else is looking—a good view of my butt. Maybe someone around here will appreciate it.

Plus, if all this guy wants is a spotter, he doesn't have to look.

I turn around with two weights in my hand, and yeah, he's looking. I smirk as I wander back toward him and slide the weights onto the bar.

But I've seen Cam look too, and so far, he seems more into this girl Harper than into me. So maybe guys just like to look at nice butts without actually being interested in the woman they're attached to. It's confusing and infuriating.

Grant pulls his shirt off before he lies down and does a few more reps while I watch his pecs ripple. He really is in great shape.

He lets out a grunt with the last rep, and I help guide the bar onto the rack. "Nice job. Thanks for spotting me." I wipe the sweat from my hands on my tiny shorts.

Grant uses his discarded shirt to wipe his forehead. "Thanks. You all done?"

"I think so. You?"

He nods. "What are you up to after this? You here with your husband?"

Subtle, Grant. "Nope. Just a friend." Now is not the time to dissect my relationship with Cam. Focus, Addie. Hot guy is flirting with you. Stop thinking about someone else. "How about you?"

Grant gives me a wink. "I'm single."

I try to subtly bat my eyelashes at him. At least, I think this is how you bat your eyelashes. Am I doing it right? I feel like I'm just blinking fast. God, I suck at flirting, if that's even what I'm doing.

Grant probably thinks I'm having a seizure.

I give up and just smile. "Well, if you need someone to hang out with this week, just let me know." I rack my weights and head for the door, wondering where on this ship Cam might be.

9

CAM

Miller told me to find a rebound, and I'm trying. Harper is an option. She couldn't have made it any clearer that she's interested. I peek into the gym as I finish off a smoothie. There seem to be a few options for a rebound in here, too, from a quick perusal.

Like the girl in black spandex. I lean against the wall as I enjoy the view of the woman bending over to place her weights on the rack. The outfit leaves nothing to the imagination, stretched tight across a perfect round ass.

As she straightens, she turns, and the red hair comes into view.

My stomach bottoms out.

That's *Addie*.

I was staring at her ass. *Shit, shit, shit.* Did she see me?

If there was any doubt before, there's none now. No more denying that I'm attracted to her, especially after I just stood here for a full three minutes and admired her ass. But there are still too many obstacles to ever consider making a move.

I back up, nearly tripping over the edge of a treadmill. Addie doesn't look my direction, thank God. I don't think I could work out with her wearing that outfit and not spend the entire time staring at her. Plus, it would be super awkward to hide an erection while I'm working out.

I turn and sneak out the door before she can see me, or before I can get upset about all of the other guys in there who are blatantly checking her out.

Except that I'm a big fat hypocrite, I realize. I was looking at her ass, like some creepy old dude. I don't have a leg to stand on here.

I'm not prepared to deal with the thoughts that are swirling in my mind as I try to forget just how nice her ass looked, how attracted to her I am. How does one explain to their best friend's sister that they're even having dirty thoughts like that? I can't admit this to Addie.

She's a sweet girl. She's too innocent, too good—

too *everything* for me. I can't put her in that position. And God, if Maddox knew I was thinking like this about Addison? I can only imagine his reaction.

I need some distance. We may be trapped on a ship, but this place is huge. There are plenty of spots I can go where I won't be tempted to do something we'll both regret.

We'll deal with the shared room when we get there. I'm not sure I can fake sleep every night.

I follow signs to the running track on the upper deck. It's pretty long, wrapping around the pool and some other areas, close enough to the side of the ship on one side that I have a great view of the ocean. I stretch my arm across my chest, feeling the tightness in my back start to loosen as the warm air brushes my face, already humid and almost sticky. A sign lists the distance and states that three laps will equal a mile. I do some math in my head, trying to figure out how many laps I want to do, then give up with a shrug.

I'll simply run however many laps it takes to forget how long I was staring at Addie's ass. I just need to focus on something other than the one thing I know I shouldn't.

I do a few stretches to warm up before breaking into a light jog for my first lap. As my muscles warm up, I pick up the speed. When I push the pace faster, the breeze is more noticeable, the mugginess mixing with my sweat. My calves start to protest, but I'm not done yet.

I'm not sure how far I've gone when Harper waves at me from the other side of the track. I should be happy to see her, right? That's generally the reaction when you see someone you're considering hooking up with. Not this pervading sense of mild annoyance.

Even with the light wind, perspiration is dripping down my back and making my shirt stick to my skin. I peel it off, dropping it on the ground in a sweaty pile as I wave and jog the rest of the lap more slowly, trying to catch my breath as I get closer to her.

"Hey, Cam," Harper says when I get within earshot, a flirty smile playing on her lips. "How's your day going?" She's wearing a pair of leggings and a tank top with the crew logo on it, the entire outfit hugging her trim body perfectly.

I slow to a stop next to her, breathing hard. "Good so far. Just getting my workout in."

Harper nods, doing nothing to hide her gaze as it travels down my shirtless chest. "Very nice," she says.

I can't tell if she's referring to me working out, or if that's her appraisal of my pecs. Or both. I choose to ignore it rather than dwell on being appraised like a piece of meat.

"What does your day look like?" I ask, stretching. I'm mildly curious what she does around here all day. Outside of hitting on the guests, which is all I've really seen her do so far.

She flips her long ponytail over her shoulder. "Mostly supervising, making sure programs are running the way they should. It's actually not too time-consuming. I don't have anywhere I need to be at a specific time." She steps closer to me. "Sometimes I slip away. No one ever misses me."

Jesus, this woman is about as subtle as a freight train. It's more of a turnoff than anything, for some reason. I fight back the urge to grimace.

"That so?" I raise my eyebrows. Part of me doesn't want to encourage her. I've never been one to go for the girls that put it all out there and make it easy. There's something about the chase, I think.

But... I told the guys I'd look for a rebound to get over Ellie, right? And I'm not really in a position to turn down a good option for a rebound, especially one with no strings attached.

Look, I know I sound like a dick right now. Or maybe it's all in my head, but I feel like a jerk for thinking about it like this. I've never been into one-night stands or hookups. It's just not me. I'm a long-term guy, or I was at one point. But the only woman

I've been with in two years is pregnant with another man's kid.

Maybe I've earned the opportunity to hook up without any strings attached. Just this once.

Harper looks down at her Apple watch. "Yeah. Actually, I have some time now. Mind if I walk with you? Or do you need to get back to running?"

I give my leg an experimental stretch. My mind has done the opposite of clearing out thoughts of Addie despite the fact that I've run so far that my quads are already sore. The stretch pulls a sharp pain from my left quad as it protests the idea of even another mile. "Walking is fine. I was just getting to my cool down."

That I wanted to do alone, in silence, but I can't bring myself to say that.

With that, we make our way around the track. After running as hard as I did, it feels as slow as an evening stroll, but we're probably walking at a reasonable pace. We pass the one other couple on the track.

I still can't get the vision of Addie's perfect round ass out of my mind. At this point, I'm not sure any number of miles will.

Harper and I make it about halfway around the track in silence before it becomes uncomfortable, and I start asking questions to break the tension.

"So, Harper. We didn't get to talk much last night.

I know you're from California and you've been working on the ship for a couple years. What else should I know about you?" I've never had to deal with finding a rebound. Do you go into personal details like this? How much do you need to know about someone that you're considering for this short-lived role in your life?

She tilts her head to the side, a few strands of hair escaping her ponytail to frame her face. "There's not a ton to know, I guess. I'm thirty-three. Divorced, no kids. Loving this single life for now. You?"

"Thirty-four. Never been married. No kids." My heart twists at that.

It's not that I'm upset that I don't have kids of my own, but more... why couldn't Ellie have gotten pregnant with *my* baby? Maybe we weren't perfect together, and with a little distance from the relationship, I realize I was never in love with her.

But even so, I would have done the right thing. I would have taken care of them. We would have figured it out together if she'd given me a chance.

I wouldn't have been as terrible a father as she suggested. My past is in the past, and I've made changes. I haven't had a drink in more than a decade.

"Good choice. I was young and stupid." She lifts her arms and drops them. "I know we got you for this cruise because you're a professional poker player, but what do you do for a regular job?"

She sounds like my grandmother. This is sounding less like her flirting and more like an interrogation. No one ever believes there's enough money in this to make it a career, but it's working for me so far.

I clear my throat. "This is my full-time job, actually. I figure eventually I'll get a regular nine-to-five job, but I'm riding this wave as long as I can."

Harper raises her eyebrows. I can't tell if she's impressed, or if she thinks this is a waste of time. I've seen both reactions. "That's pretty nice. It must be a good lifestyle, huh?"

I shrug. "It can be. I have a lot of flexibility, but it's a lot of late nights and travel for tournaments. When I settle down and have a family, I can see it being a strain."

She nods, and we walk in silence for a few minutes. I look out at the ocean. It's just miles and miles of emptiness, nothing to see but the waves.

"What would you do if you settled down?" Harper asks.

That's a good question, one I've been thinking about for a while. Everything with Ellie pushed me to think about my life in a different way.

"I have a degree in applied math and a teaching

certificate. I wanted to teach high school at one point, or even younger kids, although right now I think I might need a master's degree for that, depending on the state I work in. Or maybe I could do something in analytics. Who knows?"

Harper nods silently, pondering my answer.

I squint my eyes as we round the corner, wincing from the sun beaming right in my face. I wish I'd thought to bring my sunglasses, but I thought I'd be lifting weights in the gym until I ran away after ogling Addie's ass.

"What did you do before you started working on the ship?" I ask.

Harper looks down, her perky armor showing a small crack, and I wonder if I shouldn't have asked. Maybe people work on cruise ships to escape something. And while Harper seems nice enough, I'm not in the market for a relationship or anything deeper than a rebound on this vacation. I don't want to lead her on or make her think there's a chance for anything more than that.

She takes a breath. "I didn't work for years while I was married. I met my ex-husband while I was in college and he was in medical school. I was a nursing major. I worked as a nurse for three years while he did his residency, but then when he got a job as a full-fledged doctor, he didn't want me to work anymore. So I just stayed home."

Harper gives her head a shake, like she's shaking off bad memories, and then she's back, the carefree beach girl persona firmly in place. It's crazy how she can switch back and forth like that.

"Anyway, this is a nice deal I have going here. One could do worse than living on a ship in the Caribbean, you know? I think I'll stick with this for a while," she says with a shrug.

We walk another lap in silence while I mull over everything.

You'd think that learning more about Harper and sharing more about myself would make me feel closer to her somehow. Make me more interested in her. But I'm not, and I frown as I try to figure out why.

More people have joined us on the track by now, some walking and some running. I move to the side as a runner passes us. I know Miller told me to find a girl to hook up with and start getting over Ellie, but maybe I'm just not ready. Or is it that Harper's not the right one?

When we reach my discarded shirt, I stop to pick it up, and Harper pauses too.

"I should get going, you know, actually do my job for a bit," Harper laughs. "Thanks for talking. It was nice to get to know you a little more. Can I find you later?"

"Sure. I'll be at the pool in a little bit."

Harper flips her ponytail again. "Looking forward to it." She gives me a wink as she walks off.

My gaze follows her as she saunters away, waving hi to someone. As I focus, I realize the person she was waving to is a redhead. In black spandex that barely covers a body that's way too familiar. I curse under my breath.

Dammit, Addie really needs to change. That outfit is inviting inappropriate attention. She doesn't need guys lusting after her.

Especially me.

Addie makes eye contact with me. From this distance, I can't read the expression on her face, but she isn't smiling. I'm about to raise my hand in greeting, but before I can move, she turns away from me.

My chest tightens as she walks away, and I swallow hard. She definitely saw me, and she didn't come over to say hi.

10

ADDISON

To: AAnderson@brynmawrschools.com
From: Judy12044810@mail.com
Subject: hi its julio

hi addie mom said i can send you a letter this way are you having fun? is it warm there? are there bears where you are? mom took me to the zoo to see the bears yesterday it was fun. she says bears are not a good pet but since you're a grownup maybe you can get your own bear for your house, i think it would be fun to cuddle with a panda or grizzly bear. i could walk it for you if you need me to cause i know lots of things about bears.

love your brother julio

. . .

I see Cam and Harper the second I reach the top of the stairs, stepping out onto the deck that holds the running track. When Cam wasn't in the gym, I figured this was where he'd be.

I just didn't expect that he ditched me this morning to hang out with *her*.

What the hell is so special about Harper?

Sure, she's older than me, maybe more mature. She's got that blonde bombshell thing going for her, those tanned muscular legs, while I burn to a crisp if I'm out in the sun for too long. Plus, she definitely knows how to flirt.

And why is he open to something *now*?

I've literally been standing in front of Cam for *years*. There were times when I thought maybe he could be interested, that maybe we could have a chance. Times when I swore I caught him looking at me. But then he'd go from being friendly to being distant, and I've never understood why.

I've tried to make it clear that I'm interested, or at least I thought I did. I've never been one to brazenly flirt the way Harper seems to manage, so maybe it wasn't obvious to Cam.

Harper turns away from Cam and walks away, her

hips swaying side to side in what's clearly a practiced move. The kind of move I wish I could pull off. As she passes me, she gives me a wave and a friendly smile.

She seems like someone I could get along with, if it weren't for Cam's interest in her.

God, I sound like a jealous bitch. It feels icky.

I politely wave at Harper, then pull my gaze back to Cam.

He's watching her walk away, and then for a second, I think he sees me standing here, but he wipes his face with his shirt instead of waving. Clearly, whatever she's doing is working a lot better than what I'm doing. I tug on my hair and spin around to leave.

Maybe he's not actually into her, but it sure as shit looks like it from where I'm standing.

It just... doesn't feel good to see the guy you've been crushing on for years, the one you thought you *maybe* had a chance with this week, pass you up for someone else.

I pull my phone out of my pocket to text Annika again.

ANNIKA

> I think I need to up the sex appeal.

> What? Why? Is this about Cam again? Are you sure that's what he wants?

100%. There's a crew member who's been flirting with him and he's eating it up. If I don't try something soon, I won't stand a chance.

…But is that who you are? And how do you know he's into her?

I can be sexy!

Of course you can. You know I love you, Addie. But don't change yourself for a guy.

Maybe that is who I am. A bombshell kind of girl. Woman. Whatever.

For the record, I think this is a bad idea. He should like you for you and all that. And isn't he going to notice if you start to be all sexy and stuff? Haven't you known him for years?

I feel like I need to try something. Right now, it's just me sitting on the sidelines watching the two of them. And I want to show him there's more to me than just being Maddox's kid sister.

If it's really what you want, here's what I'd do:

> Put on that little bikini, the white one we bought last week.

> Figure out a way to get him to come in the pool with you, and a way to be near him.

> And then your bodies will be all wet and slick and pressing against one another and... fuck, this is turning me on. It'll work.

> Remember, show skin and touch. But still be yourself. Seriously.

> Perfect. Thanks. And thanks for watering the plants. :)

I slip my phone in the side pocket of my spandex shorts while I stomp away, back down the stairs and down the long hallway to our cabin.

The bikini is at the bottom of my duffel. It's a white string bikini, with two tiny triangles of fabric to hold in my average-sized boobs. Annika helped me pick it out. It doesn't have much in the way of underwire, but the coverage is so little that it doesn't matter. I was almost too shy to come out of the dressing room wearing it.

But if this is what it takes, I'm ready to wear it in public.

I pull on the bottoms and adjust the ties high on

my hips and turn in front of the bathroom mirror, which gives me a view of everything above my pierced belly button. From what I can see, it's pretty darn nice.

Cam won't know what hit him.

And if he ignores me now, I might actually hit him. In the balls.

I rest on a lounge chair in what I'm hoping is a seductive pose, my knee bent and my breasts pushed out so they look larger than they are. I'm pretty sure it's a good look for me, with the appreciative glances I've gotten from a few guys, but they're not the ones I'm after.

Cam walks up a few minutes after I settle myself on the lounger. He still has his shirt in his hand, and I'm glad I'm wearing mirrored sunglasses as I check him out.

Chiseled abs glisten with sweat. His sandy hair is wet, making it look a shade darker than usual, and it's pushed back in a way that makes it even hotter than normal. His running shorts hang low on his hips. I bite my lip; I want to lick him all over.

For a second, I wonder if maybe he's out of my league. Maybe that's really what's going on here. He and Harper are playing the game at a whole different level.

No. I push that thought away before I can get self-conscious or start to doubt myself. I've always been proud of who I am and proud of my body. I'm not going to change that now. But if he wants a flirty, sexy woman, that's what he's going to get.

"Hey, Cam," I say, pulling my sunglasses off slowly.

He looks uncomfortable, which I'm enjoying the tiniest bit. Welcome to my world, Cam. "Hey, Addie. What are you up to?"

I casually lift a shoulder. "Not much, just getting some sun. About to jump in the pool to cool off. Want to join me? You look like you've been working out."

He runs a hand over his jaw. "Uhh... sure," he says, pushing his Nikes off and tucking them under a lounge chair.

I stand and place my sunglasses on my chair. It feels more exposed to walk around like this than when I was lying down, so I slip into the deep end quickly and duck my head under water, holding the bikini in place to prevent a wardrobe malfunction.

I want to seduce him, not flash him. Or... anyone else.

When I surface, there's a splash as Cam joins me in

the pool. I float on my back, loving the weightless feel of water. This has always been my happy place, even before I started swimming competitively when I was eight. I didn't learn to swim until well after I was adopted, but I was young enough to take to it easily.

I do a surface dive to duck under the water, flipping my feet like the mermaid I wanted to be as a kid, and swim over to Cam. I surface right next to him and brush the water off my face. "Want to play Marco Polo?"

Okay, maybe not the best way to be a mature, sexy woman, but it's a fun game. And bonus—it gives me a reason to get close to him when I tag him. See? I thought this out. More or less.

Cam flashes me a genuine smile that has warmth spreading through me.

I love how he smiles with his eyes, too. I haven't seen this smile since I got on the ship, but it's one of my favorite things about him.

"Sure," he says. "Want to be Marco?"

"You be Marco first," I giggle and swim away.

He gives me a minute, then starts to move his hands out in front of him. "Marco!" he calls out.

"Polo!" I call back, splashing water in one direction before heading the other way.

He moves through the pool, trying to locate me by

my voice. I dart away but accidentally corner myself, and he catches me, brushing his hand along my arm.

"Got you!" Cam says, opening his eyes with a smile.

I push him away with a laugh. "That was too easy. Let's try again, I'll catch you this time."

Cam swims away as I close my eyes. "Marco!" I call, laughter bubbling in my voice. I'm doing my best to be mature, sexy, all that, but this is actually fun. And Cam is as into it as I am, which makes it even more enjoyable.

"Polo!" Cam calls. I swim in the direction of his voice.

I chase him around the pool for a bit, finally catching him in the shallow end. "I win!" I exclaim as I give him a hug. My arms move over his broad shoulders, and I pull myself closer, just enough to feel our bodies touch.

My skin slides over his with the slickness of the water between us. My nipples bead into hard points that I'm wondering if he can feel through the thin material of the bikini. I give it a few seconds before I push away from him.

"Your turn!" I say, trying to calm my rapid heartbeat.

I'm wet, and it's not from the water. Who knows if

this is getting under his skin, but it's sure as shit getting under mine. This might turn out to be a really bad idea if I'm the only one getting turned on.

We're sharing a room. It's not like I can masturbate in the privacy of my own suite.

Cam closes his eyes while I swim away, and we start again. It may be cheating to swim underwater with my eyes open, where he definitely can't see me, but no one ever said we were playing fair.

I circle around him a few times, just out of reach.

"Marco!" Cam calls out. He's facing away from me.

I give it a second before I respond. "Polo!" I splash more than I mean to when I go to dart away.

There's another splash, bigger than mine, and when I turn to see what it is, Cam is right there. He wraps a strong arm around me and opens his eyes. "Got you," he says, smiling as he pulls me into his hard body. "Think you're good at this game, huh?"

What game is this? I can't think. I can barely breathe.

The only thing I can focus on is Cam's muscles as they press against my body. The muscle of his arm ripples as he holds me tight against him. This bikini is so thin that I'm no longer wondering if he can feel the hard points of my nipples. I know he can.

And I can feel a bulge in his shorts. I'm not the only one turned on here.

I let my legs drift open, one falling on either side of one of his legs. His thighs are large, spreading my legs further than I'd expected on either side of the hard muscle.

We're so close. All it would take is one lean to bring my lips to his. Another few inches and his leg would press against my sex instead of my thigh. My heart beats faster in my chest, pounding so hard that I'm sure he can see my pulse jumping in my neck as my smile dies and my lips part, waiting.

It feels fast, too fast, but it's what I've dreamed of for so long. My breath hitches in my throat.

"Cam," I whisper. His pupils dilate as I watch, my gaze fixed on his face.

11

CAM

The urge to pull her even closer hits me. Her body fits so perfectly against mine, soft in all the right places. Her tits are up against my chest, her nipples hard even through her bathing suit, and somehow my leg is between hers.

All I'd need to do is—

Wait. What the fuck am I doing? Letting Maddox's little sister press her scantily clad body up against mine? That's a quick way to hell for sure, even ignoring the thoughts I'm having now. Because he's told me, oh, a million times that Addie is off limits.

And worse, I'm realizing I want to do more than hold her close, which is absolutely out of the question. I can't kiss her. I can't run my hands down her body, no matter how hard the thought makes me. I can't picture her naked or imagine doing all the things I'm imagining doing right now.

Maddox is my best friend, practically my brother. I owe him more than to scam on his little sister.

And Addie is way more than a rebound.

That thought is what snaps me out of it. She's off limits in so many ways, but the reality is, Addie Anderson is not the type of girl you have a rebound fling with. She's the kind of girl you fall in love with, the kind you want by your side forever.

For that kind of girl, you take things slow. Not like this.

I overcompensate by moving her arms and pulling myself away from her a little more forcefully than is necessary. "I'm going to sit in the sun for a bit," I say gruffly, heading for the edge of the pool.

Addie follows me, climbing out of the pool just after me. I have both the pleasure and pain of watching her lift her body out of the water, droplets cascading over her gorgeous tits that are barely contained in that scrap of fabric she's trying to pass off as a bathing suit. She looks like a goddamn Sports Illustrated swimsuit model.

I look away, then peek back. Just for a second. Because I can't help myself.

Addie settles on the lounge chair to my right, still

dripping wet. Her bikini is practically see-through, but it wasn't exactly covering much in the first place.

Dear Jesus fuck, I really can't get a boner right now. I was already starting to get hard in the pool, when Addie pressed up against me. Thank God for the cool water, because I'm back down, but one look at her and I'm sporting a semi.

"You okay, Cam?" she says, peering over at me.

"Yes," I say, but it comes out sounding strangled. I cough to clear my throat. "Yeah. I'm fine."

If a completely inappropriate case of blue balls counts as *fine*. And putting aside the fact that I'm a terrible person for the thoughts I still can't chase out of my head.

Addie perches on her side, facing me. Dear God, please don't let her breast fall out of her bathing suit. I'll never be able to get that out of my mind. "You just seem... strange, I guess. I thought we were having fun."

We were. And God knows I've wanted to touch Addie like that for a long time. But she knows we can't, right? Not because I don't want to. Because if I start, I won't be able to stop myself. And we just... can't.

From the way she's looking at me, though, I can tell she's not going to let it go.

Then again, I've known Addie practically forever.

If she's on a path, there's no dissuading her or subtly changing her mind. Being direct is the only thing that works, and even then, the chances are about fifty-fifty.

I let out a sigh. "Addie, you're a sweet girl." More than sweet. She's fucking perfect. "I just... we can't play that way."

She arches a perfect eyebrow. "What way, Cam? We can't play in the pool together? Or you just don't want to touch me?"

Fuck. This is not going well. I can't think about touching her. "Addie, Maddox is my best friend."

"And?" she presses, not backing down.

I blow out a breath, leaning forward to put my elbows on my knees. Can't she have mercy and put me out of my misery? "And I feel like I owe it to him to look out for you, as his little sister. That's all. And part of that is making sure guys don't take advantage of you." *Including me.*

Addie doesn't respond. She lies on her back, one knee up. She slides her sunglasses on and leaves her hands above her head. This move pushes her chest forward, in case I wasn't already doing everything in my power to avoid looking at her breasts.

The worst part of all of this is that I know Addie. I've seen her in this mood before. Under her innocent exterior, she's stubborn and won't give up on what she wants.

She can try, but she won't get away with it on my watch if I have anything to say about it. But I know that even as I think that, this might be a losing battle. Because I'm not fighting this because I don't want her. I'm fighting it in spite of the fact that I do.

This was supposed to be a reset. Maddox and me on the open seas, just two bros having fun. Not me and his sister embroiled in a tangled web of emotion that can only end with one or both of us getting hurt.

I let out a sigh as I settle into my own lounge chair, hoping I'm reading too much into this. Maybe Addie is just messing around or hoping for some fun while we're on vacation. Maybe there aren't real feelings mixed up in this, which is just even more reason to stay away from her.

Addie Anderson is not the kind of girl you hook up with. She deserves more.

"Enjoying the sun?"

I open my eyes to find Harper sitting sideways on the lounge chair to my side.

Addie and I have been sunbathing in silence for

almost thirty minutes. Every few minutes I open my eyes to check on her, but she hasn't moved other than to adjust herself slightly on the chair. She's going to end up with a wicked sunburn if she didn't put sunscreen on.

It occurs to me to say something to her, but I can only imagine how she'd take it. Yeah, I'll keep my mouth shut. I'm kind of attached to my balls.

I shift to face Harper, brushing a hand through my hair. It's almost dry after sitting in the sun, the pool water leaving it in a messy, spiky configuration. "Yeah. It's a beautiful day."

Her blonde hair swishes in her high ponytail as she tosses her head. She's in her crew uniform—not the outfit she was wearing this morning, but the white collared shirt she had on when we boarded the ship. "Just wanted to stop by and say hi again. I should do some actual work around here, but I wanted to see if you were up for a drink tonight, or maybe dinner? I can find you in the dining room or stop by the casino."

I'm acutely aware that Addie is listening to every word of this conversation. I shift further toward Harper, trying to sort out the best way to address this tactfully and without getting either of them pissed at me.

I give Harper what I hope is a friendly smile. "Sure.

I'd love to." It can't hurt to get a soda at the bar. Addie can't get mad at me for that, right?

Harper rises from the chair, tossing that ponytail over her shoulder. "Can't wait."

She meanders away, pausing to chat with a few other people on her way out of the pool area.

Addison whips her sunglasses off and sits up as soon as Harper is far enough away that she can't hear. *Oops.* I pretend I don't notice the fire in Addie's eyes, but it's hard to miss.

"I'm going for a walk," Addie announces, sliding those cutoff jean shorts on over the string bikini—*don't focus on her ass, Cam*—and slipping her feet into sandals.

"Aren't you going to wear a shirt?" I ask, trying to keep my voice level.

I'm trying to think of something to say that doesn't reference her perfect ass, but the second the words leave my mouth, I'm regretting them.

Not that she doesn't look good. She looks too good.

Long legs extend from the frayed edges of her shorts, which are barely long enough to cover that butt, which has already spent too much time living rent-free in my head today.

And now that I'm thinking about her shirt, I'm

focused on her top. The scrap of fabric she's claiming as a bikini barely holds her lush tits in, but provides enough support for some truly impressive cleavage. She looks hot.

"No," she says, her voice curt. She turns on her heel and struts away.

My gaze follows that perfect round ass as it moves from side to side until I catch myself and force myself to look away.

Get it together, Allen.

12

ADDISON

To: AAnderson@brynmawrschools.com
From: karen_a_morgan@mail.com
Subject: SAT math

Miss Anderson,

Rudy says you've informed him that math is, indeed, on the SATs. As such, we'd like the tutoring you're doing for him to cover what's necessary for him to do well, as we'd like for him to be able to play football at an Ivy League school. Could you start on those lessons this week?

Thanks,

Karen Morgan

I'm fuming as I stomp away.

Those moments in the pool we were so close to—well, something. Obviously not sex, since we were in public. But there was a spark, wasn't there? There was this electricity, this tension between us. He had to have felt it.

And then he pulled away. Not just a normal backing up, even. He couldn't get away from me fast enough. He practically jumped out of the pool. And then to flirt with Harper right in front of me? I mean, I get it—she's all skinny and tan with her perfect blonde hair and the way she sways her hips when she walks, but it almost seemed like she was doing it on purpose.

What the hell, Cam?

I was worried that my yelling at him last night would be interpreted as a tantrum, yet another strike in the Addie's-too-young column or whatever other reason he's using as an excuse to stay away.

But it didn't seem like he saw me that way when we were in the pool. For about half a second, I thought there was a chance.

Some people would view this as a loss. But I'm playing the long game. I place my bets, then let it ride. I straighten my shoulders as I walk and lift my chin.

Something affected him. *I* affected him. I smile to myself. *It's a start.*

The ocean breeze sweeps across my chest as I tuck my phone into my back pocket and lean over the railing of the ship, ignoring the emails from work as I remind myself that I'm on vacation. I physically can't tutor Rudy this week since I'm out of town, but somehow telling his mom *no* feels too confrontational.

The warm touch of air reminds me that this bikini is really leaving the girls on display. The sea stretches endlessly towards the horizon. It gives me hope.

If I can't see land, I have time.

The sheer number of things to do on this cruise ship is amazing. So many places to be on my own; I can simply avoid Cam for a few hours while he gets his shit together.

Decided, I grab some lunch at one of the little cafe options, a chicken salad wrap and some barbecue flavored chips that I munch on while I walk along the deck and watch the ocean. The movie theater is showing one of my all-time favorite movies, Sleepless in Seattle, so I spend a few hours there before wandering around the ship again for a while.

I'm feeling a bit more relaxed now. Maybe I'll even take a trip to the spa, get a massage or something before I have to get dressed for dinner and get ready to work in the casino tonight.

Last night, Cam and I both worked as dealers, but tonight he starts the gig he was really hired for: teaching people strategy and how to play poker well. I just get to deal for him. I haven't decided if it's good or bad that we have to work together.

Pro: More time with Cam, with the ability to brush up against him frequently and try to get him to notice me.

Con: If Harper shows up and he flirts with her, there may be no stopping Hurricane Addie.

That's what my family called it when I was a teenager. You've heard of the famous redhead temper? Well, it exists. When things would set me off, I'd storm through the house, targeting anything or anyone in my way.

In my defense, they kind of goaded me on when I got in those moods.

But no Hurricane Addie this week. I can hold it together. I'm a cool, collected, mature woman who is worthy of a man's attention. Specifically, Cam's.

My hours of wandering the ship's decks have done wonders for my ego, at least. It turns out when you walk around in practically nothing, it does indeed draw men's attention. So I've got that going for me. I'm not the most experienced in this brazen flirting, so it's nice to see it's working in some ways.

Just not with Cam, apparently.

I sigh as I watch the unchanging horizon.

"You look like you're deep in thought," a voice behind me says.

I look up to find the dark-haired man from earlier in the gym. He has a cleft in his jaw that makes him seem rugged, even in a Hawaiian shirt that has the top two buttons undone.

I give him a smile. "I was. But I'm happy to be interrupted."

"Addison, right? We met earlier in the gym. I'm Grant." He holds out his hand, and I take it.

"I do remember you. Good to see you again."

He smiles, revealing a row of almost too-perfect white teeth. "I don't want to disturb you, if you were contemplating something important. But if you're not locked into your musings, I'm looking for a partner for some of the lawn games they're playing down there." He motions behind me. "You interested? It's silly stuff, cornhole and shuffleboard and things like that."

Cam is on the upper deck, still at the pool as far as I know. And I've done enough brooding for the day.

The idea of playing some low-stakes games seems like a great way to take my mind off of things with Cam.

I flash a beaming grin. "You know what? That sounds great."

I've learned a few things about Grant since we started playing:

1. He's really bad at cornhole. I think he's missed every shot he's taken, and I'm carrying the team.

2. He's definitely interested in me. He's flirting and finding every possible excuse to touch me. Unlike Cam, who couldn't get away from me fast enough.

3.

There is no number three. That's all I've learned. But that's all I need to know. He's cute, single, and interested. All perfect ingredients for a vacation fling. Right?

I'm feeling better about myself after Cam's brush-off, too. This is an attractive guy, around my age, single, and he's into me. There isn't the same spark or tension that I feel with Cam, and I'm not totally sold on hooking up with Grant. But all I wanted was to know that I'm desirable, and Grant has already confirmed that.

I heft the beanbag in my hand, balancing a cocktail in the other, and toss it underhand, watching it arc through the air and hit the board, sliding a few inches before it drops through the hole.

"Nice shot!" Grant puts an arm around my shoulder and squeezes.

I grin up at him. "Thanks. All up to you now."

He groans good-naturedly and picks up a beanbag. "This is going to be the one. Wish me luck." He leans his face down toward me. I plant a kiss on his cheek, mostly because it seems awkward not to.

Grant lets the beanbag sail through the air, making a perfect arc to land two feet beyond the target.

I laugh. "Oh, well. It's a good thing I don't like you for your cornhole skills."

He joins me in laughter. "Good thing. How are you doing with your drink? Need another one?"

I look at the plastic cup I'm holding. It only has a few sips left, so I tip it back and drain the rest of the cocktail. "Sure. Another one would be great."

Grant winks at me and heads to the bar.

I pull my phone out of my back pocket while I wait.

ANNIKA

> I'm flirting with a guy! I think. He seems into me, at least.

> Things working with Cam?

> *frown emoji* No.

> You found someone else already?
> Jesus, Addie.

> Is it bad if I just want to flirt with him
> to make Cam jealous? Or to make
> myself feel better?

> Is that what you're doing? He's a
> human, Addie, or I assume he is. He
> has feelings too.

> Crap. He's coming back.

I slide the phone back in my pocket and accept the drink Grant hands me. It's strong when I sip at it, and I'm already feeling tipsy. I'll have to pace myself.

"At the risk of embarrassing myself further, do you want to play another round? Or they have some beach volleyball, shuffleboard..." Grant looks around, biting his lip. "And ping pong. Any interest?"

I take another sip. I'm not sure beach volleyball is the best idea right now. My tits are barely contained as it is, and while I'm enjoying the ego boost from Grant's flirting, I don't want to lead him on. Annika has a point there.

"Let's play ping pong," I suggest.

He holds out a hand to help me up from the beach chair I sat in while I was waiting for him to come back with our drinks, and he keeps holding my hand while we walk over to the tables.

After Grant's poor showing at cornhole, I was expecting to carry the team, but he's actually good. Like, *really* good.

I, on the other hand... let's just say racquet sports aren't my forte.

I swing the paddle as the ball comes toward me and completely miss, almost hitting Grant with the paddle instead.

He's grinning, amused, as I come back with the ball.

"How are you so good at this?" I grumble, hitting it back toward our opponents.

He bats the ball easily as it comes his way, a clean shot that scores us a point. "I played tennis in college." He shrugs.

"Where did—" I break off as the ball comes to my side. I make contact this time, and the ball flies over the tiny net and lands somewhere beyond the table. Rats.

"Maybe we should go back to corn hole," Grant

laughs, watching the other team go searching for the ball.

I shrug, smiling. "Or we can find something we both suck at."

He laughs as the other team serves the ball.

Ultimately, we lose with only three points to our name, all of them scored by Grant, of course. Can't say I'm not impressed.

"You want to sit and talk?" Grant motions to some lounge chairs.

"Sure." I follow Grant in that direction. He bypasses the main sets of chairs, settling himself instead on something that looks suspiciously like a bed.

Grant kicks off his sandals and leans back against the pillows. "Glad we grabbed one of these. The daybeds are always taken."

I chew on my lip. This is moving a little fast. But then again, I said I wanted a vacation fling, didn't I? And we're in public. Nothing is going to happen... right?

I slip out of my flip-flops and climb onto the bed next to him, far enough away that our bodies aren't touching.

Grant laughs as he lounges, putting one arm on the pillows behind me. "Afraid to get too close to me?"

If I had any doubt that Grant was looking for a

vacation fling too, it's gone now. But now that we've moved from easy flirting while engaged in another activity to this one-on-one, I'm feeling a little uneasy. Not like he's a bad guy or anything, obviously. Just... he's not the one I really want.

But then, that's the point of all this, right? Moving fast. We have limited time. It's not like I'm going to date him after all this, so we don't need the slow burn, the buildup, the will-he-won't-he spark of uncertainty.

Which, honestly, is disappointing, because that's the best part of romance novels and, by extension, romantic relationships.

I'm torn as I lean away from him, just a little. I want a whirlwind romance, the spark and passion and all that stuff you see on TV and in the books. But I want something real. With Cam, it could be. A frown plays on my lips, one I have to fight to hide.

Is it too much to wish that I could have all that on this once-in-a-lifetime trip? Are my expectations *that* unreasonable?

I don't see any of that with Grant. I'm about to excuse myself when another voice breaks in, sinking my stomach and putting me on the defensive with four words.

"What the fuck, Addie?"

13

CAM

I've been looking all over for Addie for almost an hour. I figured I'd give her time to cool off before I came to apologize, but I didn't think I'd find her like this.

The guy she's following onto the daybed reminds me of the wolf in Little Red Riding Hood, luring his prey closer and closer.

He does the high-school move where you put your arm on the back of something, behind the girl you're with and then let it slowly migrate down to her shoulders. It was sleazy then, and it's sleazy now, especially if you're a goddamn adult.

I storm over toward them, anger clouding my vision. Maybe he's a nice enough guy, and maybe he's not actually trying to get in her pants, but right now

I'm not in any mood to give him the benefit of the doubt. I don't know what game she's playing, but this isn't the kind of guy she should be spending time with. I'm not sure I want her spending time with any guy, to be honest.

"What the fuck, Addie?" I snap as I close in on them.

Addie looks up at me, her mouth falling open.

The guy she's with puts a hand at his forehead, shading his eyes from the sun as he looks at me. "Hey. I'm Grant. You know Addie?"

Damn right I know Addie.

"Yeah. We've got somewhere to be, though. Let's go." I motion to her.

She looks between me and Grant, then finally slides off the edge of the daybed. "Bye, Grant. Let's hang out again soon."

She gives him a wink—*a goddamn wink*—as she picks up her shoes and walks away ahead of me, and I'm almost certain it was entirely done for my benefit, not Grant's. It's like she's trying to piss me off. And it's working.

Can you spank adults? Because there's nothing I'd like more than to pull this little brat over my knee and tell her to get her shit together.

"Addie, what are you doing?" I ask when I catch up to her. "Who the fuck is that guy?"

Addie whirls on me, the same fury in her eyes as what I saw at the pool, when Harper stopped by. Guess the time to cool off didn't work the way I was hoping. It seems to have been simmering instead, ready to boil over.

"I'm doing what I want, Cam. He's a guy I met. None of your business." She pushes open the gate of the activity area, walking out onto the main deck, flip-flops still in her hand.

"Put on your shoes." I avoid the main topic, saying the first thing that pops into my mind.

She plants her hands on her hips, narrowing her eyes. "Or what, Cam? I'm not a six-year-old. You might think you're here to keep an eye on me, but I'm an adult and I can do what I want. Like walk barefoot. Or flirt with guys."

I cringe. *Shit.* That wasn't my point. I panicked, okay?

The last thing I want to do is treat her like a little kid. I want to protect her, but one look at her body and it's clear—*excruciatingly* clear—that she's an adult.

When we get to the door of our cabin, Addie is even more fired up than before, if that's possible. I brace myself. I've had the dubious pleasure of watching Addie in action when she's furious, and it's mildly entertaining when you're not the target.

When her fury is focused on you, however, it's terrifying.

"Addie, I'm just trying to look out for you. I care about you, you know that. I just don't want you to do something you regret." Dear God, I hope reason will eventually win out here, but I have my doubts.

As soon as the door shuts, I know I'm right. There's no reasoning with her. Addie's volume increases exponentially once we're in the privacy of our own suite.

I've been a witness to a handful of Hurricane Addie occurrences, but never the target. Looks like that's about to change.

"Camden Allen, it is not your job to take care of me like I'm a goddamn teenager or kid you need to monitor. If you don't want me, fine. But you can't keep me from dating at all!"

She stamps her foot and takes a step toward me. I open my mouth to tell her it's not that I don't want her, but the words freeze in my throat.

Addie's shirt is in the middle of the floor, and as she steps toward me, one foot lands on the shirt while a toe of her other foot hooks into the fabric, sending her pitching toward me.

I react instinctively, my hands going out to keep her from falling, and I catch her in my arms, holding tight.

She's shaking while I hold her—from anger or the adrenaline rush of falling or something else, I'm not sure—and breathing hard. I keep my arms around her, gripping her to my chest and do my best to ignore my own racing heart and how right this feels.

How perfectly she fits.

How warm and soft and solid and fragile she is, all at the same time.

How easy it would be to kiss her, if she tilted her head the tiniest bit.

Addie's wrong. It's not that I don't want her. I do. I can't, though. Not even the brush of my lips over her head that I want to offer for comfort.

Instead, I grit my teeth and force myself to wait patiently until her shaking eases a bit, then let her go and take a step back, away from temptation. My anger has dissipated. All that's left is a need to protect her. I'll do whatever it takes to make Addie happy, I realize. Even if it leaves me miserable.

"You okay?" I ask gently. "Sorry for grabbing you. I didn't want you to fall."

She shakes her head, but no words are said.

"You're not okay?" I look her over for injuries. Maybe I let myself get too lost in her. *Dammit, Cam. You're supposed to take care of her. Not paw at her like that.* "Did I pull too tight? Shit, Addie, I'm sorry." I never should have grabbed her that way. What's wrong with me?

Addie blows out a breath while I'm still talking. "I'm fine, Cam. You don't have to apologize," she mumbles.

A wave of relief rushes over me that she's alright. "I do, though, Addie. I shouldn't be touching you like that. Not when you're wearing..." I motion at her outfit. One breast has nearly escaped its confines in the fall.

Addie looks down and adjusts herself while I do my best to look away, aching to touch her again. "What's so wrong with me, Cam?"

"Huh?" I'm not sure I understand the question, because there's nothing at all wrong with her. She's so fucking close to perfect it astounds me that no one has taken her off the market yet.

"Why are you so repulsed by me that you can't even touch me? Grant is obviously interested. What's so wrong with me that you won't even look at me?" The anger is there, but it's fading, and there's an undertone of something else taking its place. Pain or vulnerability, maybe?

My voice softens. "Addie, nothing is wrong with you." *You're perfect* is what I want to say, but even I know that's crossing a line.

She huffs out a breath. "I'm a grown-up, Cam. Who my brother is has nothing to do with who I can sleep with."

Not what I was going for. I suppress a groan. "Addie, I—"

"What, Cam? You don't want to think of me dating? Sleeping with someone? Is that it?" she fires back.

That's exactly it, in fact, but I'm not sure saying that would go over well. "He's my best friend. You're his baby sister. You were like thirteen the first time I met you, for Christ's sake." How is she not getting this?

"He's not even my real brother. We're adopted. You know that."

I sigh. "Addie, that's not the point here."

"So, what is the point? I'm twenty-seven years old, Cam. You can obviously flirt with whoever you want. Why can't I?"

"Jesus, Addie. You can flirt if you want. I just... I don't want you to get hurt, that's all. You don't know this guy." I'm not sure how to end this conversation, this fight. I hate fighting with Addie, but if she needs to get things off her chest, I can at least do that for her.

Addie's eyes are blazing, a flush rising in her cheeks. For a second, I let myself wonder if this is what she looks like in bed, when she comes. When she's screaming a man's name.

A muscle twitches in my jaw. I don't want to think of her screaming anyone's name but mine.

She crosses her arms over her chest. "Cam, get a grip on reality. I'm a big girl. I can take care of myself."

Addie spins around and stalks toward the bathroom door while I stand there, trying to find the words to explain my reasoning. I'm the one in control here. I'm in the right.

She looks over her shoulder, door in hand. "Now, toss me some clothes. I'm going to change. In here, so I don't offend your fragile eyes."

I open the closet and pick a t-shirt and shorts off the tops of the piles of clothing. I check to make sure they'll cover her enough so that I don't need to pluck my eyes out, then toss the clothes her way.

She catches them easily and looks at what I've supplied. A scoff blows from her lips. "No underwear, huh? Guess I don't need any." She slams the door.

I sink down on the small sofa, wincing at how hard

it is. I don't want to think about Addie's underwear. Or her not wearing underwear. Jesus, fuck.

I realize with a start that there's no winning here, is there? Either I have to go through her underwear or put her in a situation to wear none.

No winning for me, I mean. Either option is meant to torture me. She's obviously the winner, if people can win at a fight like this.

Shit. Where does this leave me? And where does it leave the two of us? If this were any other girl, Maddox is who I'd be turning to for advice. But he's away on his honeymoon, and I'm not going to intrude on that. Miller would just make a joke. Blake is firmly anti-romance at the moment.

And if I can't be objective about Addie, there's no way in hell any of the guys can. Especially not Maddox.

The fire seems to have died down a little when the bathroom door opens again. Addie is in the t-shirt I picked, but she's twisted it up into something that bares her abs. The shorts are low on her hips, and all I can think is, *She's not wearing underwear.*

I really need to get a grip here.

I take a breath. "Addie, I'm sorry. I'm not trying to be a dick. Let's back up here."

She pauses in the doorway. Her arms cross over her chest, but she doesn't argue.

I sit on the sofa and pat the seat next to me. "You can talk to whoever you want. I just care about you, and sometimes I go overboard."

She slowly crosses the room and sits. "I have an overprotective brother already, Cam."

She has a point. And I already know that pushing for her to stay away from other guys is going to have the opposite effect, and trying to stay away myself isn't working. Plus, this is Addie. I've known her forever, and I actually like hanging out with her.

Maybe I'll be stuck with blue balls, but the least I can do is spend time with her as friends.

"How about this, then. Friends? Let's explore Nassau together tomorrow. We can have fun and not worry about anyone else," I suggest.

She twirls a strand of red hair around her finger and tugs on it. "Okay."

I hold back my sigh of relief. "Were you planning to hang out with that guy? The one you were with when I found you?"

Addie shakes her head with a shrug. "I just met him. We were just hanging out, Cam. There wasn't anything between us, and there was never going to be. We don't even have concrete plans to see one another again."

For some reason, this makes me very happy. Actually, who the fuck am I kidding? I know exactly why it makes me happy. It's because I can't shake this insane idea that Addie is mine, even if I can't do anything about it.

I clear my throat. "Well, if you're okay hanging out with me, we can find something fun to do. I don't want to just explore the island alone."

She tugs on her hair again, and I have to stop myself from pulling the strand out of her fingers and wrapping it around my own fist. "You're not going to spend the day with Harper?" she mumbles.

"I wasn't planning to. And even if she asks, I'd rather spend the day with you, Addie."

Addie looks at the ground. "I think she likes you."

I nudge her with my elbow until she looks at me. "Hey. Harper can like whoever she wants. It doesn't mean I have to reciprocate."

And given a choice between spending a day with Harper and spending time with Addie? Easy decision.

A smile plays on her lips. "Okay."

"Good. Now, let's talk about stuff to do in Nassau."

14

ADDISON

To: AAnderson@brynmawrschools.com
From: SusannaC123@mail.com
Subject: tests?

Hi Miss A,
Did you grade our tests from last week yet?
Hope you're having a good break?
Suz

To: AAnderson@brynmawrschools.com
From: JoBloom@mail.com
Subject: Grades

Miss Anderson,
Hope your vacation is going well. Can I meet with you
after school next week? I got a really bad grade in
English class, and I don't know what to do about it.
Joanna

"Can I get you a drink?" Harper says to Cam, ignoring me. She's in a little black dress, and even I can admit she's stunning. I can see why Cam is interested in her, even though it still pisses me off.

He's been on his best behavior since our fight. So have I, to be honest. We have to spend several hours together here in the casino tonight, and this would be *really* awkward if we weren't speaking to one another. But we've made amends for now.

Not only did he apologize, but he also offered to pay for us to go on one of the excursions they peddle to tourists visiting the island.

There are a ton of options—snorkeling, glass-bottom boat tours, ziplining—and I feel like I could spend a week there without ever doing the same thing more than once. By the time we had to show up tonight in the casino for our poker gig, it was between snorkeling and an ATV tour.

Either one sounds amazing to me. I might be leaning *slightly* toward the ATVs, because there are no sharks on land, but I'll let Cam make the final call since he's paying for it.

Despite Harper's obvious flirting, Cam seems a little more immune to her charms this evening compared to earlier today. She's standing—posing, almost—with her hip jutted out, one hand placed just below her narrow waist while she waits for him to answer.

Cam, for his part, has only glanced at her, keeping his attention squarely on the cards. He's easygoing, but he takes his responsibilities seriously.

"I'll just have a soda, thanks. We're going to take a break in a bit and maybe then we can talk." Cam peers at the cards as I deal out a new round. He lays his hole cards—the two in his hand that are unique to him alone—out on the table, face-up, so the other players can see what he's working with.

Normally, he'd keep them a secret, of course, but his goal in playing tonight is to teach the other guests how to play poker like a professional.

Harper walks off toward the bar, and Cam looks around the table.

"Now, I have a four of spades and a king of clubs. The king is a high card, so I'll consider that, but they're not matched in suit and not close enough to be part of a straight. Typically, with a hand like this, I'll match the blind but not raise big in the first round," he explains.

The players look between Cam and his cards and the cards in their own hands, all tossing chips into the center.

Cam continues to direct the game. Really, he could do both our jobs by himself.

"Now, Addie is going to deal the flop. That's the first three community cards. Remember, you can use zero, one, or two cards from your hand in combination with any of the community cards to make your strongest five-card hand."

I lay three cards out on the table as Cam narrates.

"So, we're seeing a queen of spades, two of diamonds, and two of hearts. This isn't giving me much to work with. When you combine these three with my cards, the best I have now is a pair of twos—but so does everyone else at this table. Typically, I'd fold here, but for the sake of our lesson, I'll stay in."

He pushes a chip in front of him. Unlike at the other two tables tonight, this is just a lesson, so there was no buy-in, and the chips aren't actually worth anything.

The other players follow his lead, and I lay down the turn card.

"A two of spades. Now, this is interesting, because it increases the chances that someone has a full house, which is a great hand. Someone may have four of a kind, even."

They don't. No one has a good hand. I'm no professional, but even I can tell that all of the players are just staying in because it's free. Not a single one would have called the bet after the flop if their chips were worth anything.

Harper reappears after a few moments holding two drinks in her hands just as I turn over the river—the last community card—to reveal a two of clubs. What are the odds of that?

Cam raises his eyebrows in surprise, focused on the game and completely ignoring Harper, which makes me the tiniest bit happy. "Wow, four of a kind. Super rare to have this kind of a deal, you guys. Can anyone tell me how we'll sort out the winner? And what hand you should use?"

The players lay out their hands, any illusion that we're actually betting on this vanished. After each hand, we pass out the chips again to make it yet another even playing field, so it's not like it matters.

The man to my left scratches his beer belly as he looks at the cards in front of him and back to the community cards before he smooths his comb-over. "I have a full house with three of the twos and my pair of fours. Is that good?"

Cam nods toward the poster showing the rankings of poker hands. "It is good, but that wouldn't be the best hand you can make. What do you think, Susan?" He looks at the next player. I don't know how he remembers all their names.

From the interactions I've seen between the players, I think Susan is married to comb-over guy. She's also way out of his league, if I'm being honest.

Susan taps a finger on her jaw. "Well, I'd say four of a kind. And my highest card other than that is the queen right there."

Cam nods. "Good. Four of a kind with a queen kicker."

He looks at the other players, two young men who are clearly very much in love and also very much cheating by looking at one another's cards. I hide a smile as the taller one leans over to analyze his partner's cards.

"Four of a kind for both of us. Ace high for me.

Tyler has a jack high. So does that mean I win?" Tyler's partner asks.

"Indeed, it does. So, when you get a rare deal like this, with four of a kind in the community cards, it comes down to who has the highest card in addition to the four of a kind. Congratulations." Cam motions toward the poster. "The only hands higher than four of a kind are a straight flush or a royal flush, which no one would have with four of a kind showing."

Harper has been quietly standing a little too close to Cam, watching this all play out while she sips her drink.

Cam gathers the chips together. "Let's take a break. If you'd like to gamble for real money, there are two other tables open. If you're up for more lessons, come on back here in, say"—he looks at the clock across the room—"ten minutes."

The players vacate the table while I reshuffle the cards.

Harper slides into the seat next to Cam and hands him a glass. "I got you a Jameson on the rocks. You seem like a whiskey kind of guy." She grins.

I can't read the expression on Cam's face, but he pushes it back toward Harper. I'm not sure he is a whiskey guy. I've never seen him drink at all, now that

I think of it. He's never made a big deal of it, but he's also never talked about it, at least to me.

He puts on a polite smile. "No, thanks. Just a soda is good for me. Or a water."

"Aw, come on," Harper whines, nudging him with her bony shoulder. "Live a little, loosen up. It'll make things more fun later."

A muscle ticks in Cam's jaw. "No, thank you."

Harper is either oblivious to Cam's mood or is simply choosing not to care. "I just want to have fun with you tonight, Cam. Having one drink won't hurt. Come on."

Being a high school teacher, I'm familiar with this kind of peer pressure, but we're well past that stage. It's not cool anymore. I'm not sure it ever was, to be honest.

Cam turns and looks her square in the face. There's an edge to his voice I've never heard before. "Harper, I said no thank you. I think you should find someone else to have fun with tonight." He stands and walks away.

My eyes widen at the blatant rejection. Do I go with him? I look at Harper, wondering if I should say something, but she looks unaffected by Cam's blowoff. She takes the glass she brought for him and tips it back, draining it in one sip before she stands and walks off without saying anything to me.

Guess I know where I stand with both of them.

I keep shuffling cards to give my hands something to do, my gaze wandering around the room. Cam is by the bar, holding a glass of something that looks like cola. Even from across the room, it's obvious how tightly he's gripping the edge of the bar with his other hand.

He seemed fine before Harper brought him a drink. Did I miss something?

He was fine when we headed to the casino tonight. He was fine while we were playing, even when Harper first showed up. His mood seemed to turn when she brought him the drink.

"You look like a natural with the cards."

I startle at the voice and look up to find Grant standing next to me. He cleans up well. The scruff I remember from earlier in the gym is gone, and he's clean shaven. He looked good in workout clothes, but the slacks and golf shirt he's in now are even better suited to him. He's attractive by any definition.

But despite all of that, I still don't feel a spark. Not like with Cam.

I give him a smile anyway. I can be friendly without encouraging anything. "Hi, Grant. Thanks. I've been playing cards a long time. My friend and I are actually giving poker lessons tonight, if you're interested. He should be back in a few minutes, and we'll start a new round."

Grant nods thoughtfully, bringing a wine glass to his lips. "I'm not sure he was the biggest fan of me, honestly, but thank you for the invitation. So, do you have to stay at the table? Would you be able to get a drink in a little bit? I was enjoying getting to know you earlier."

Dammit, he's cute. And single. And interested. Why can't I be into him? Why do I have to be so hung up on Cam?

I sigh internally, glad that I can at least hold it together on the outside. "It was nice getting to know you, too, Grant. But... I'm not really looking for something right now. My personal life is complicated."

It makes me feel even worse that he's not angry or upset.

Grant just smiles, nodding wistfully. "Well, thank you for being honest. I can't say I'm not disappointed, but I understand. You'll make some lucky guy very happy one day, Addison." He lifts his glass in a mock toast, then turns and saunters away.

I watch his retreating form for a minute, then look back to Cam at the bar. He seems to have relaxed a little, and he's smiling and laughing with the bartender. My heart warms at the thought of spending all day with him tomorrow.

I shuffle the cards again and bend them in a bridge as they snap back into place.

Tomorrow is my big chance. All day with Cam. And it might be my last chance. Because once we get back on board after our day in port, we'll be in Miami by the next morning.

It's now or never.

15

ADDISON

To: AAnderson@brynmawrschools.com
From: JosieChrisAndersonFleming@mail.com
Subject: Favor

Hey Addie,
When are you going to be back in town? Chris and I
are in town house-sitting and watching the dog for
Maddox and Holly while they're on their honeymoon.
We would love to see you. Have a favor to ask, too.
Love you!
Josie

We're scheduled to dock in Nassau this morning. When I wake up, we're already here. I swing my legs over the side of the bed, feeling for the ladder with my feet before shimmying down.

Cam was nice enough to pay for an excursion for the two of us, and even though I'm pretty sure he just feels bad that I can't afford one on my own, I'll take it.

Because I really, *really* want to make the most of this day.

Getting to hang out with Cam is just the delectable cherry on top.

I peek at his bed, finding him still snoring, which is for the best since I'm not wearing shorts—just a pair of bikini briefs under my tank top, my only PJ option this week. He'd better get up soon, though.

I grab my outfit for the day before I duck into the bathroom and get ready.

The plan is to sightsee in the morning and check out the markets and other tourist destinations. The afternoon is going to be spent doing an ATV tour of the island. I've never ridden an ATV, but Cam assures me it's basically like a high-powered golf cart, and therefore something even I can handle.

It's not that I'm a *bad* driver. It's just easy to get

distracted by conversation or changing the music or looking at the deer on the side of the road. And I've never been in a car accident for real. Just a popped tire from hitting the curb too fast, and the time I accidentally went the wrong way down a one-way street.

No one else was on the road. It was fine.

I look through my clothes in the closet and settle on a pair of soccer shorts and a t-shirt. It's cute enough to walk around, and sporty enough to hike or get dirty on the ATVs.

Pursing my lips, I tap my finger on my chin. Should I bring anything? I shouldn't need much for the day, but I grab my backpack just to be on the safe side. I don't want to have to come back to the ship if I don't have to, and I'm sure things like sunscreen are marked up beyond belief in a tourist destination like this.

I toss my phone in alongside the Coppertone, an extra shirt just in case, and my wallet with my passport tucked inside. That should be enough. I'm not even sure I need my wallet, since I know Cam isn't going to let me pay for anything today, but there's always a chance he'll let me buy him a beer or some lunch. The information from the cruise said we didn't need passports to get off the ship, but to bring it when we leave.

Cam wakes up with a snort and a groan as I zip the backpack. "What time is it?"

There's the Cam I know. Not a morning person by any stretch of the imagination.

When he and Maddox would stay at our house during college breaks, he'd never appear until 10 a.m. or later, usually bleary-eyed and searching for coffee.

I'm not exactly a morning person either, at least not all the time. But if there's something exciting going on, the adrenaline is better than coffee, and I can be up-and-at-em with even the earliest of early birds.

Cam isn't one of the grumpy types... most of the time. He just looks bleary and confused until after he's brushed his teeth, which is better than hostile, like my freshman roommate. I woke up at 5 a.m. to take a shower and get going one day when we were supposed to head up to the mountains to ski, and she locked me out of our room while I was in the dorm's communal bathroom.

"Almost nine. We just docked, but since our ATV thing isn't till this afternoon, you can sleep in more if you want," I sling the backpack onto my shoulder. I'm ready to get going, even if Cam isn't.

He rubs the sleep out of his eyes. His scruff is thicker in the morning, bordering on the beginning of a true beard. I wonder what he'd look like with a full beard. If anything, the thickening scruff makes him look hotter.

Like a sexy lumberjack. Mmm. I wonder if he owns any flannel.

He runs his hand over his jaw as he climbs out of bed and makes his way to the bathroom.

And I only peeked a little, honest. You would, too, if your crush was walking past you in nothing but boxer shorts that prominently displayed a bulge. He clearly did his best to tuck away what must be morning wood, since he's not pitching a tent in there, but it's still pretty obvious. And it is by no means small.

I settle on the couch, scrolling through my phone while Cam does whatever boys do in the bathroom. I know I take my sweet time with makeup and hair products and such, but he seems to spend longer than I do.

It's a mystery to us all.

My phone contains email after email, mostly spam. I delete them one after the other, painfully aware as I do that this is faster than unsubscribing from all these lists but it's not going to solve the underlying problem.

There are also a bunch from work—so much for teachers getting spring break off, right?—and from everyone else I know, all of whom seem to need things from me.

I huff out a breath. I hate putting off helping people, but this is supposed to be my time. Right?

It's no different from any other time in my life. And usually I love feeling needed, even if it's inconvenient. But I'm on vacation, so they'll have to wait. Even Rudy and his SAT math crisis.

I shake my head. If he doesn't know enough math to pass the SATs as a junior in high school, he might have bigger problems than passing a now-optional test and staying on the football team.

I lock my phone and drop it back in the bag without answering any of them except Julio. I love that kid. He's really blossomed since mom adopted him last year. I make a mental note to bring him something from Nassau.

Then I have a moment of guilt and open my phone again to respond to messages from work. Just a few. And the one from Josie. If she needs a favor while I'm on vacation, it must be urgent. Probably. It better not be about avocados again.

Cam finally emerges from the bathroom looking like his usual self. He's shaved back down to just a bit of scruff on his chin, and he's styled his hair somehow so it looks messy, but not just-woke-up messy. The effect is attractive as fuck, and he makes it look effortless.

If I didn't know any better, I'd think he rolled out of bed looking like that and not like the crazed guinea pig that I saw walk into the bathroom.

He gives me his signature lopsided grin. "Ready for a day of fun?"

"Yep!" I hop up and sling the bag over my shoulder. "Ready."

The air is humid and fragrant with the scent of something sweet—pineapple or some other tropical fruit. The island is surrounded by the bluest water I've ever seen. I always figured those pictures were photoshopped, but it's one hundred percent real and amazing.

After two days on a ship, the ground feels unsteady under our feet, but the feeling goes away as we walk toward the center of the city.

The island is dotted with multicolored buildings, with new things to find everywhere. We wander through some of the open-air markets, looking at handmade items and souvenirs.

I end up buying a bracelet made of conch shells for Annika to thank her for plant-sitting and bowls—also made of conch shells—for my mom. Then I grab some colorful woven scarves for my sister Josie and her wife Chris. I also pick out a tote bag for Holly.

I'm still looking for things to get for Maddox and Julio. And maybe the twins?

Josie and Chris's little ones are only ten months old, so I'm not really sure they'd even understand at this point. Maybe t-shirts or something.

"What about this?" I hold up a hat woven out of some kind of straw.

Cam looks over his shoulder. "It's cute. For you?"

I study it again. Maybe it does look a little feminine. "I was thinking for Julio. Maybe not?"

He shrugs. "Maybe keep looking? If you don't find anything better, you can always come back."

I take his advice and continue on in one direction while he goes the other, checking out stall after stall of colorful goods. Right at the end, I see it. There's a stall filled with wooden carvings, with a man seated in front of it whittling a new figurine. And right in the middle, there's a whittled bear figurine. Julio would love that. A bear of his very own.

The man is busy wrapping the bear in tissue for me when a warm hand lands on the small of my back, sending tingles to the base of my spine.

"I got a lead on somewhere for lunch," Cam says. "It's supposed to be awesome. Kind of out of the way and they don't cater to tourists, but I think it's worth walking to. You up for it?"

We follow the complicated directions Cam was given. I stick close to his side as we eventually come upon a tiny cafe that's definitely not listed in any of the guidebooks. The paint is peeling on the building, the chairs mismatched.

It looks like a hole in the wall, which usually means it has the best food.

"What should we get?" I ask, keeping my voice low as I look over the creased menu with an eager grin. "Are there things the islands are known for?" We stick out like a sore thumb, the only tourists in the place.

Cam looks over his menu at me with a wink. "You trust me?"

"Yeah. Of course. Just don't feed me something gross." I wrinkle my nose.

I'm not the most adventurous when it comes to eating. I try to be open-minded, but I don't like when things are too bland or too spicy. Or things that have a weird texture, like escargot or cow tongue. Bleh.

I once dated a guy who'd studied abroad in France, and he swore cow tongue was the best thing he'd ever had, and he made it for me.

It was most definitely *not* the best thing ever.

In fact, I still can't get the chewy-mealy texture out of my head. I shudder at the memory.

Cam plucks the menu from my hand and sets it behind his. When the waiter comes over, he orders for both of us, only looking at me when the waiter asks what we'd like to drink.

I'll admit I'm skeptical, but when the servers cover our table with dish after dish of steaming, fragrant food, all my misgivings are gone. This looks amazing.

"How do you know what to order?" I ask, helping myself to something fried. I dip it in a pale orange sauce that looks suspiciously like the concoction my sister-in-law Holly likes to put on fries and pop it in my mouth, letting out a little moan as the flavors burst on my tongue. "Oh my God. That's so good."

Cam digs into another dish, putting a square of pasta on his plate. "I looked it up before we came. These are all things that are supposed to be Bahamian specialties. This is their macaroni and cheese. Then we have conch fritters, which is what you just tried. Then conch salad, Johnny cake, and boiled fish."

I reach for the conch salad. I've only heard of conch in relation to their shells, the ones that so many things in the market were made of. I didn't realize there was some kind of meat inside. But the fritters were so good, and the second I try the salad, I'm hooked. The conch meat almost reminds me of calamari in its texture. It's delicious, light, and almost sweet.

The waiter sets drinks in front of us—a soda for Cam, Malibu and pineapple for me. I take a sip, closing my eyes to savor the tanginess. It goes perfectly with the food and the feeling of the island.

I can see why people go on vacation to places like this all the time. It's too bad we only have today to spend here. There's so much to explore.

Maybe someday I can save up enough money to come back here for a few days. I make a mental note to look into the cost of flights to and from the Bahamas. Maybe Annika would come with me. We could lay on the beach, drink Mai Tais and Rum and Cokes and Malibu and pineapple all day and spend every evening eating conch fritters.

I down more than my fair share of the food by the time we have to leave the restaurant. I hope it all stays down while we're on the ATVs. They can't be that bumpy, right? I cross my fingers.

All the food was just too good to leave on the plate, and now I'm so full that if I burp, some of my lunch may reappear, but it was a risk worth taking.

Jesus, then Cam would *really* be turned off. We're finally in a good place, getting along and friendly, even though the sexual tension simmers just below the surface, at least for me. I don't want to jeopardize our closeness.

My sense of direction is abysmal, so I let Cam lead us back through the marketplace—the one he swears is the same as the one we were just at, even though I only recognize a few stalls—and to a sign that announces that **ATV TOURS START HERE.**

The guides outfit us with helmets and get us settled on ATVs, one person per vehicle. I pull my hair back into a low ponytail before I settle the helmet on my head. It's heavier than I thought it would be, and the musty smell inside blocks out the smell and sounds of the island. I feel like it would keep my skull from cracking in a collision, which I suppose is the point.

I rap it with my knuckles to make sure. Cam, of course, sees me do this, and takes the opportunity to sling his arm around my back and knock on the helmet, too. I squeal and try to push him off of me, but I don't push very hard. I'm enjoying his body being close to mine, the vibration of his body against my own as he laughs.

The vehicles seem more or less self-explanatory; hit the gas to go, the brake to stop, turn the handle bar to steer. Got it. I turn the key in the ignition, and it roars to life, the loud motor startling me.

I swallow over the lump in my throat. It's okay. We're okay. There's a kid who looks younger than my students in our group. I can handle this.

We turn off the main road, away from the palm trees and view of the ocean as we follow the group of twelve tourists following one tour guide. Another one brings up the rear behind Cam and me. We follow a trail that heads into the woods, the tree canopy providing shade that feels refreshing in the heat. The gap between me and person ahead of me soon grows wider, but I'm afraid to go too fast. Cam is patient, sticking right behind me. He doesn't tell me to hurry up, and I could hug him for it.

I'm finally getting the hang of this, at least at low speeds, as we come to a hill. It's steep, and my ATV isn't making much progress with my foot light on the gas. I take a breath and push down on the gas.

The ATV jolts forward, climbing the hill. I glance back at Cam, a smile stretched across my face. How does he look hot even with a huge helmet on?

But then the vehicle lurches as it hits something.

I turn back just in time to see the ground rushing up toward me.

16

CAM

My adrenaline is pumping as we maneuver the ATVs through the island, slowing down to see things: the trees are different here from what we have in Pennsylvania, and if I squint, I can see the ocean through the greenery at some spots. A group of flamingoes looks at us as we pass.

We hit a wide-open expanse and I speed up, pushing the pace. I'm having the time of my life, even going a little slower at Addie's comfort level.

We reach a hill, and it takes her a minute, but then she realizes she needs to give it a little more juice to make progress. She gets it going and turns back to smile at me. I smile back, but the expression dies on my lips as the ATV Addie's driving jerks when the tire hits something on the path. The vehicle goes skittering sideways, turning.

My heart nearly stops completely as Addie tumbles off, rolling once, and the ATV lands on its side only inches from her body. The sickening sound of crunching metal hitting the ground sparks a memory, and my heart plummets to my feet.

I can't hold back the curse that escapes from my lips as I hit the brakes. "Addie?"

I shift my ATV into park and climb off to sprint over to her. She's not moving. My heart races in my chest, and my breath catches in my throat as fear floods through me at the sight of her small, still body.

The guide behind me pulls his vehicle to a stop next to us. The rest of the group is so far ahead they can't even see us anymore.

"Addie. Are you okay?" I crouch down next to her, one hand on her shoulder. I need her to be okay.

She blinks her eyes and sits up, shaky. Relief washes through me. "I-I think so. I think I hit something, and..." She puts a hand to the shoulder that impacted the ground, and when she pulls it away, there's blood on her palm.

"You must have landed on something. Let me see."

I tug her bloodied shirt out of the way to see a gaping wound on her upper arm that makes me wince. Shit. "Addie, that looks really bad." I glance at the guide. "Is there a hospital around here?"

He nods, shielding the sun from his eyes with his hand. I take her backpack from her and sling it over my shoulders as I settle her in front of me on my ATV, making sure her helmet is still secure.

"I've got you," I say, wrapping one arm tight around her waist as I grip the handle with the other. Addie's hand lands on mine, soft and trusting, and I hold her tighter, pulling her back against my chest. "I've got you," I say again.

We follow the guide down the path, much more slowly than before. I'm doing my best to avoid rocks and sticks, trying to keep the ride as smooth as possible so I don't hurt her more.

The absolute terror of seeing her fall still hasn't completely gone away. It wasn't the reaction you have to a friend or a little sister or anyone you don't have strong feelings for. I push the thoughts to the back of my mind, unable to process them for now. I'm barely ready to deal with the fact that I'm attracted to Addie. Feelings like *this* are something else entirely.

I'm grateful she was at least wearing that helmet.

There was a small dent in it that I can't get out of my mind. I can only imagine what would have happened if she hadn't been wearing one.

The hospital is only about ten minutes away on the ATVs, even going at this slower speed. It's a small building, but modern, and Addie gets called back after only a few minutes in the waiting room.

Her injury is still oozing small rivers of blood down her arm as she stands, and I sit back in my chair. I want to follow her—need to, almost. Not just to distract myself from the memories that conjure up from the smell of disinfectant—my head throbs with a phantom pain—but to make sure she's okay. To take care of her.

Addie takes a few steps after the nurse, then turns back to me. "Will you come with me?" she asks softly.

Thank God. I practically jump out of my chair. "Of course," I say. I don't want to let her out of my sight. I catch up to them and follow the nurse, my hand on Addie's lower back to keep her close.

We walk through a swinging door, and we may be in another country, but the fluorescent lighting and sterile feel is a universal hospital thing, not to mention that sharp smell. It's been over a decade since I last visited an emergency room, and the scent makes me feel like it was yesterday that I was getting stitches of my own.

We're led to a small room, where the nurse directs Addie to sit on the bed while she checks her heartrate and looks at the cut.

The woman purses her dark lips. "This looks like it may need stitches. The doctor will be in shortly, and they can let you know for sure, okay? You can hold this on it while you wait if you'd like." She hands Addie a small cloth. Her accented English is the only thing that reminds me we're not in the US right now.

I sit down on the doctor's stool while I wait with Addie, rolling it to sit by her.

"I'm sorry," she says, biting her lip.

My brows furrow. "For what?"

She shrugs, then winces as that makes her injured arm move. "Messing up our day. Having to spend our day in port at the hospital. This isn't exactly what I meant when I said we should check out the local culture."

I chuckle and climb off the stool to sit beside her on the hospital bed. "Well, this is one way to get a firsthand view of what it's like to live here, I guess." I nudge her good arm and tilt my head. "It's not a problem though, Addie. I'm having fun just hanging out with you. We got a lot in today already. I'm just sorry you got hurt."

She flushes slightly. "I'm a pretty terrible driver. Maybe I should have warned you."

I shake my head, biting my cheek to keep from laughing. She may be a bad driver—I've witnessed it firsthand—but this one wasn't her fault. "This one isn't on you, Addie. ATVs are supposed to go over anything. I'm sure you just hit something, and it was a freak accident. I'm just glad the ATV didn't land on you."

She pales at the idea. "Was it close?"

I close my eyes, reliving the scene I can't get out of my mind. "Yeah. Too close."

"Oh." She swallows. "I guess I'm lucky that just my arm got hurt."

The doctor chooses that moment to walk in, a stethoscope draped around his neck. I stand up, leaving Addie alone on the bed as the doctor asks her all the same questions the nurse did before examining her arm. When I get a closer look as he pulls the cloth away, I see it's a deep wound. She must have hit a rock or something when she fell.

"I'm going to have to stitch this up," the doctor announces in the same accented English as the nurse, sitting back. "I'll numb the area, so you won't feel anything."

Addie winces. When he comes back in with supplies, she gives me a pleading look until I move closer. She clings to my hand in a vise-like grip while the doctor works, not letting go until he secures a bandage over the area.

"Now, you'll need to have the stitches taken out in ten to fourteen days and monitor it to make sure it doesn't get infected. Ibuprofen should be enough for the pain, but I'll give you a prescription for a few tablets of something stronger, just in case. There's a pharmacy on the way out where you can fill it."

Addie nods as she takes everything in.

"Now, avoid using that arm as much as possible. Are you right-handed?"

Addie shakes her head. "Left-handed. I'm the only leftie in my family."

I can see the realization dawning that her dominant hand is the one attached to her injured arm. Her expression immediately darkens.

The doctor continues his instructions while scribbling something on a chart. "Ah. Well, you may need to have help with some things for a day or two so you can rest your arm to let it heal. Are you and your boyfriend staying on the island for long?"

We both quickly shake our heads.

"He's not my boyfriend," Addie says, just as I interject, "We're leaving today."

The doctor looks amused but visibly works to hide his smile. "I'll get your paperwork ready so you can head out. Enjoy your vacation."

He exits the room, and Addie and I glance at one another.

"I'm not sure I'm going to be able to deal tonight at the casino," she says.

I sit down next to her. "That's not a problem. You just take it easy. I'll help you out."

She wraps a lock of hair around her finger, using her right hand for a change. "I'm sorry, Cam," she mumbles.

I take her hand, forcing her to release the hair. "You said that already. And it's fine. There's nothing to be sorry for."

"Okay. Thank you." She looks down at her shirt, the sleeve torn and covered with drying blood. "I brought an extra shirt. It's in my bag. I don't know why I thought I'd need one, but I guess it's a good thing I packed it. Can you grab it from my backpack?"

I pick up the bag from where it's resting on the floor and undo the zipper, then place it on the bed between us.

Addie shuffles through it and pulls out a shirt. "Go out there while I change." She motions to the hallway with the shirt in her hand.

"Um, Addie," I say gently, "you might need help."

She cranes her neck to look down at the bandage. "Shit."

I let out a small laugh. "Yeah. It's not exactly convenient."

She chews on her lip. "Um. Can you help? If you don't mind. I don't want it to be weird."

"It's not weird, Addie. You don't even have to ask. It's fine." I take the shirt from her and shake it open to find the Phillies logo looking back at me. "I didn't know you were into baseball."

"Yeah. I don't really follow it, but I like going to games. Hockey, too."

I pull her uninjured arm through the sleeve, then pull it over her head before finally sliding the shirt off the injured arm while she talks.

"Sometimes I go just to enjoy the food at the stadium, you know? I don't always even watch the game. When I was little, we went a lot as a family, because tickets were cheap back then, but since they won the World Series, it's gotten more expensive." Addie keeps talking, almost a stream of consciousness that I've seen her employ before when she's nervous.

I do my best to focus on being a good guy, the kind she can trust. Not the kind that looks at her cleavage while her shirt is off. Because I'm realizing why I'm having trouble looking away. Why I couldn't breathe when she fell.

I have feelings for my best friend's little sister. And I don't know how much longer I can fight them.

The clean shirt goes on in the opposite order that the first one came off. I tug the hem down to her waist, making sure she's fully covered.

"Baseball season is starting soon, too. I should look into tickets for a game," she says, still rambling.

I lean forward and plant a kiss on her forehead before I can stop myself. "There. All better."

That stuns her into silence, and she just nods, cheeks flushed pink.

I take the papers the nurse hands us and help Addie to her feet. She slings the backpack over her good shoulder, and we make our way to the exit, stopping to pick up her prescription. When we leave the hospital building, the sun is nearing the horizon, and those little pink and white houses cast long shadows across the ground.

I look around for a clock. We were supposed to be

back at the ship at 4:30, and I'm getting a sinking feeling that we might be cutting it close. The ship leaves at five.

Addie pulls her phone from the backpack. "It's 6:10. Shoot. We're going to be late."

"Yeah," I say, going through the options in my mind. We're not going to be late. The ship is going to be gone.

"We should hurry, right? We don't want to miss it." She starts to walk quickly—in the wrong direction, I would like to point out.

"Addie. Stop."

"Hurry up, Cam. We'll get in trouble if we're late, right? We have to do the thing in the casino again tonight." She doesn't even look back.

I jog to her and grasp her shoulder to slow her to a stop. "Addie. First, you're going the wrong way. The ship docked over there."

She lifts her hand to her forehead, blocking out the rays as she looks into the setting sun.

"And second? The ship is gone. It left at five. Remember?"

Her jaw drops open. "Fuck. What do we do now?"

I shrug. One more disaster in my life.

But as I look at Addison, I realize I'm missing something. That usual feeling of a pit in my stomach when the rug is pulled out from under me yet again just... isn't there. Stress isn't forming a ball, twisting my insides into a knot of unease.

For some reason, I don't think I mind being stuck here with Addison. Almost like if we're together, everything is going to work out okay.

And that's the strangest feeling of all.

17

ADDISON

To: AAnderson@brynmawrschools.com
From: karen_a_morgan@mail.com
Subject: Re: SAT math

Miss Anderson,

I haven't heard back from you on tutoring for this week? Since there's no school, Rudy has a lot of free time, and we would like to use some of that to work on his math skills. Can you get back to me on when you can do that?

Thanks,
Karen Morgan

To: AAnderson@brynmawrschools.com
From: JosieChrisAndersonFleming@mail.com
Subject: Re: Favor

Hey Addie,

Can you watch the twins Sunday? I want to take Josie out for her birthday, somewhere where we can go without highchairs and baby food. Judy is busy doing something with Julio. Please, please? We're staying at Maddox and Holly's house (I think Josie mentioned we're house-sitting/dog-sitting. The dog might need therapy after a week with the twins). Feel free to bring a friend along; they're a handful. Would love you forever.

Chris

My jaw is still hanging open. We missed the ship. It's somewhere in the Atlantic Ocean, far away from us. With my clothes and my makeup and my hair products on it, not to mention my underwear.

Now what?

I'm starting to hyperventilate when strong hands grip my shoulders. "Addie. Breathe."

I do, and I lift my gaze to see Cam staring intently at my face. "What do we do?" I stammer, barely able to string together anything more coherent than that.

He doesn't move his hands. It feels comforting, like he's this strong presence I can lean on. I'm freaking out about being stranded on this island, but with Cam here, I think it might be okay.

Maybe. But I really need a hairdryer.

"Look at me," he commands.

I focus on his eyes. The blue looks almost green in this light, with little flecks of gold that catch the sun. My breathing steadies as I keep my gaze there.

"Good. Now, we're going to find somewhere to stay for the night. Then we'll figure out a flight home. I can get in touch with the people from the cruise, and maybe they can ship our things back." He lets my shoulder go and pushes a hand through his hair. "You brought your passport when we left the ship, right?"

I did. It's tucked into my wallet, just like the guidebook recommended. My muscles relax the smallest bit. At least we're not trapped on the island. I nod, and Cam mirrors my movement.

"Good. I have mine, too. We'll need them to fly home from here."

I twirl my finger in my hair, taking a deep breath.

It's not the same to do it with my right hand, but my left arm hurts when I lift it too much.

"I'm sorry," I say. "This is all my fault, isn't it? If I hadn't gotten hurt, we wouldn't have had to go to the hospital, and I wouldn't have needed stitches and we wouldn't have had to wait for the doctor and everything, and we wouldn't have missed the—"

I'm cut off as my words are suddenly muffled by a large chest. Cam pulls me close, avoiding putting pressure on my injured arm, and holds me tight.

"Shh. It's okay. None of this is your fault. And it's okay. This just means we have extra time in Nassau." He murmurs the words into my hair, his voice vibrating through me.

I let myself relax against him. The steady *lub-dub* of his heart is soothing, consistent. I use it to guide my breathing. *In, two, three, out, two, three.*

Cam doesn't move for several minutes. I'm vaguely aware that we're standing on a public street in the middle of Nassau, with me clinging to him for dear life, but my world has been boiled down to just the two of us.

"Are you ready for me to let go?" Cam says eventually.

I nod, and his grip loosens, but he keeps one arm around me as he turns us the opposite direction from where I was headed. "Let's head this direction. We should be able to find a hotel around here."

Spring break in the Bahamas is not a good time to walk into a hotel and ask for a room. We try two different hotels before finally finding one with vacancy, and it's a fancy one.

I wince as we enter the lobby. I'm not sure I can afford this. There's a bubbling fountain at the center of a massive lobby, and the paintings on the walls look like they cost more than my monthly salary. Yearly, maybe. I cross my fingers that they won't have any rooms.

"We have the Presidential Suite available, or we have a standard room with two queen beds or one king," the woman at the desk announces, looking between Cam and me.

"I, um." I clear my throat. "What's the price for a night in each of those?"

The woman looks at her computer screen. "The Presidential Suite is a thousand a night. The—"

"We'll take the room with two queen beds," Cam cuts her off as he slides a credit card across the counter.

"Very good, sir," she replies, typing on the

keyboard in front of her. The tap-tap-tap of the keys echoes in the expansive marble lobby.

I elbow Cam in the side, glad he's standing on my right.

"Ow! What?" He looks down at me.

I give him a death glare.

"What?" His brow furrows. "Do you not want to share a room? I figured it would be okay since we've been sharing the room on the ship. If not, we can get two rooms."

God, men are clueless. "I can't afford this place," I hiss, darting a glance at the woman who's clearly pretending she can't hear us.

He raises a brow and shrugs like it's nothing. "So? I'm paying for the room. And that's why we're sharing. It'll be fine."

I'm going to murder him. Forget the whole crush I've had on him for, oh, thirteen years.

"Here you are!" the woman says brightly, handing two cards to Cam. "Breakfast is complementary. The outdoor pool and lounge are open until 11 p.m., but the bar out there closes at nine. After that you'll have to visit the bar in here." She gestures to the bar across the lobby.

"Thanks," Cam says, pocketing the keys.

"Enjoy your stay!" she beams with a practiced wave.

I hold my anger in until we're in the elevator. The second the doors slide shut, I whirl on him. "What the hell, Cam?"

He looks unconcerned. "What, Addie? We need a place to stay tonight. I got us one. It's fine. Calm down."

He did *not* just tell me to calm down.

"Camden Allen, you fu—"

The elevator doors open, and the curse dies on my lips as a family with two small children hurry in. I clench my jaw.

The family gets off on the same floor as us—*fuck*, I need to yell right now—and they disappear into a doorway close to the elevator. Cam uses the key card to open a room further down the hall, and as soon as the door shuts, Hurricane Addie unleashes.

"You fucking asshole! Do not tell me to calm down. We're *stranded* in a foreign country, and we don't have extra clothes or toothbrushes or pajamas or a hairdryer. This is a *disaster*. My arm hurts like a motherfucker. My boss is trying to get me to be the senior class advisor because whoever has been their advisor for three years isn't up for planning prom. My sister is trying to rope me into something when I get back. I forgot to water the plants in my house. Rudy is going to fail his SATs, and his mother is going to blame me. I don't have extra shoes. Or makeup. Everything is a *mess*." I stop to take a breath.

Cam sits on the edge of one of the way-too-luxurious beds. "Okay. What else?"

"I—" This takes the wind out of my sails. What *else*? No one has ever responded to Hurricane Addie that way. They just want the crazy lady to stop yelling.

I study him, but he's nodding in a sincere way.

"I just... I feel like everyone wants something from me lately. And I can't say no, because then I'm not happy, agreeable Addie, and I *want* to help, but sometimes it's too much. And I feel really out of control right now, and I don't like it. And..." I pause. "That's it. I think."

"You sure?" Cam asks. Again, he doesn't look like he's mocking me, the way my sister used to. He's not wincing the way my mom does when I go on a rant like this.

I breathe out, slowly nodding. "Yeah. That's it."

"Do you want advice? Or just to vent?" he says, startling me.

What *do* I want? "I... I think I just needed to vent." I look at him. "Thank you."

He gives a short nod and stands, placing his hands

on my shoulders. "Okay. Let's see what you packed in your bag and what's in the bathroom, then we can see what the hotel will give us for free. Fancy places like this sometimes give you free toothbrushes and shit like that."

For the first time in my life, Hurricane Addie doesn't end with slamming doors and more tears and everyone in a bad mood. It doesn't end with people mocking me or me feeling like some out-of-control kid that's ruining everything. It just... ends. Without judgment.

"A-ha!" Cam emerges from the bathroom, holding something aloft. "A hairdryer!"

We have a late dinner in the hotel restaurant, where we stuff ourselves again on conch fritters. It's one of the things the island is known for, and for good reason. I think I could eat these every day and be deliriously happy.

We close ourselves back in our room after dinner. I flop on the bed furthest from the door, my stomach full.

"Hey, Addie?" Cam says, sitting on the edge of the other bed.

"Ugh. So full," I groan, patting my belly.

"Can I use your phone? Mine is on the ship. I want to see if I can find flights home."

I turn my head and point to my backpack on the floor. "It's in there. Give me a minute, and I'll grab it for you."

He picks up the bag and carries it to the bed while I manage to sit up. I unzip it and go through the contents, handing the phone to him after I unlock it.

Looks like I'm down to some sunscreen and my wallet. In retrospect, I wish I hadn't packed so light, but I suppose the essentials are my passport and things in my wallet. And a phone. I'm not sure how we'd book flights without it.

What did people do for travel before apps?

Cam taps on my phone for a few minutes. "I can get us on a flight tomorrow at 5 a.m., or the next day at noon."

Cam at 5 a.m.? Yeah, right. And while the idea of being here one-on-one with Cam has me a little nervous, it's not any different from what we were doing on the cruise, not really. Plus, this might be my one and only chance to really experience the Bahamas. I'm not sure I can make a trip like this happen again any time soon.

I bite my lip. "Honestly? If you're okay with it, we

could do the next day. Maybe enjoy one more day here in Nassau. Then you wouldn't have to wake up super early."

One side of his mouth lifts in a smile. "Yeah. Good point." He taps a few more things. "There. We're booked. And now we have a whole extra day to enjoy. What do you want to do tomorrow?"

I look down at my arm. The injury is going to put a damper on things, that's for sure. "I think maybe just the beach or relaxing at the pool. I can't do too much more with my arm. But if you want to—"

Cam is already shaking his head. "I just want to hang out with you, Addie. Today has been really fun, the hospital visit aside. I don't need to do some crazy adventure thing. Let's do the beach or the pool or both, and some good cocktails. Sound good?"

A smile spreads over my face. "That sounds amazing."

"Good. Now, get your ass over here and let's watch a movie or something before bed."

I climb onto the bed next to Cam. He helps me fluff the pillows behind me, so I don't have to use my injured arm, and once I'm settled, he hands me the remote.

"Pick a movie. No porn." He gives me a pointed look.

I snort as I start to flip through channels, pausing at Hallmark. I honestly love their movies. They're predictable in a good way. Boy meets girl, they fall in love, everyone lives happily ever after. I bite my lip and scroll past it, though. Cam probably wants something more manly.

"Wait, go back," he demands.

I look at him, confused. He can't be serious.

"What was that one on Hallmark?"

I click back a few channels. "You don't have to watch a Hallmark movie for me, Cam. It's okay."

He leans over and slings an arm around my shoulder to pull me close, then plucks the remote out of my hand with a grin. "I love these movies. Please?"

He wasn't lying. Cam is more into this movie than I am. I'm enjoying it too, though, and about halfway through I realize I've relaxed into the bed enough that I'm pressing into Cam's side.

Memories of our time in the pool come flooding back. The heat of his body against mine, his strong arms pulling me into him. And the utter humiliation when he pulled away from me and gave me a lecture about how we can't play like that.

I shift to move away from him. I'm having a good time just being with him, and I don't want to ruin it. If there's any chance for us, I'm realizing it won't come from me pushing him.

But when I create space between us, Cam's arm moves, circling around my back and under my injured arm to pull me closer without taking his gaze off the movie. My stomach flips, and all the blood rushes to the area between my legs, leaving me lightheaded and almost dizzy.

I can't read too much into this. Can I?

I try to look up at him to figure out what he's thinking. With his arm around me, I'm flush against him. It's solid, comfortable. Safe.

He looks back down at me, and something in his eyes is different. He reaches his free hand across us to brush a lock of hair out of my face and tucks it behind my ear. The move shifts his body so he's almost above me, still cradling me with his arm.

Cam smiles down at me. "Hey."

18

CAM

I'm a complete goner.

I've known Addie has had a crush on me forever. I've never given it much thought or encouraged it both because of my relationship with her brother and because she's so much younger than me.

Even as I've noticed her more and more over the years since she turned twenty-one, I've kept my distance. But seeing her on the ground today when she fell from her ATV? I haven't been scared like that in a long time. Maybe ever, actually.

It's one thing to get in an accident where you're the only one hurt. It's another thing entirely when someone you care about is hurt. And it's making me realize there's something more there. Something more to these feelings between us.

Even on the ship, I was doing my best to keep our relationship on the straight and narrow. Convincing myself that it's just lust and not worth the risk.

But something is different now. Hell, everything is different. I'm not sure I can pinpoint when it started to change exactly, but it's clear as fucking day now. And I think something has changed for her, too.

"Hey," she whispers back. The movie is completely forgotten. Her eyes widen beneath those insane lashes, long even without the help of mascara. She may have been worried about leaving her makeup behind on the ship, but I love her natural beauty.

I run a finger down the side of her cheek to her jaw. My thumb rubs over her lower lip. "Can I kiss you, Addie?" I ask, my voice quiet in the shadows of the room.

She darts her tongue out to run over her lip, and it catches on my thumb. *Fuck.* My balls tighten. I want to push my thumb into her hot little mouth, feel her suck on it and imagine it's my cock. But this is Addie. I need to take things slower. She deserves better.

She nods, a slight movement of her head.

I slide my fingers to gently pinch her chin and lower my lips to brush over hers. Soft, sweet. I want her to know I want this, but also that she's in control here.

I'd never take it further than she wants. If this is as far as it goes, I'll stop right here.

But when I pull back and look at her, her eyes are heavy, the pupils dilated so far that the honey-brown of her irises is a thin rim. Her breathing is shallow, quick.

"Cam," she breathes, swallowing hard.

"More?" I rest my forehead on hers.

"More. Please."

I shift us again, pulling her down on the bed until she's practically lying flat, and I lean over her, balancing on my elbow. I run a finger along her hairline.

"I'm sorry I've pushed you away, Addie. It was never about you," I murmur. I want to tell her about Ellie, about my past, about all the shit that's been going wrong in my life, but all I want to think about right now is Addie.

"Why?" she asks.

"Because you're Maddox's sister. Because—"

She shakes her head. "I know why you pushed me away. But why... why did you change your mind? Are you sure?" She bites her lip.

I press my thumb to her lower lip to pull it from between her teeth. "Because I can't stay away from you, Addie. I want you. I want everything with you. And I can wait if you're not ready."

She shakes her head again, but this time she doesn't say anything. She slips her arm out from where it's been pinned between us and pulls me down to her. Her fingers fist in my hair as our lips meet, firm and insistent this time.

I run my tongue along her lips. I need to taste her, to know all of her. She parts her lips, and I slip my tongue inside her mouth.

It's sweet, like pineapple and something that's just *her*. From one taste, I know I'll never have enough. She meets me, her tongue diving into my mouth, and we tangle together. I pull back to take a breath and she holds me tighter against her, her teeth closing on my lip before she finally lets me go.

"Shit, Addie," I pant, my mind racing just as fast as my heart.

She presses her hips up against my groin. I'm so hard it's painful, and I let out a groan as she grinds against me.

"Take your pants off," she says.

I search her face for any hint of uncertainty, but there's only lust. She wants this just as much as I do. I push away from her and stand next to the bed while I undo my belt and shove my boxers and jeans down in one motion, freeing my erection before I pull my shirt over my head.

"Holy shit," Addie breathes.

I try to hide my smirk. Yeah, I know I'm big. But I don't know how much experience Addie has, and I don't want to hurt her. From the way she kisses, though, I don't think she's a virgin.

She lifts her hips to shimmy her shorts off. Then she pauses, and her cheeks flush. "Um. Shit. Can you help with my shirt again?"

I lean over her from where I'm standing. "Getting to peel this shirt off you is one of the sexiest things I've ever done. I'll undress you any time, baby."

The flush turns an even deeper crimson, but she sits up and lets me help her. I take my time tugging the Phillies t-shirt up and over her head and down her injured arm. I let my thumb brush over the swell of breast that rises from her bra.

The shirt lands on the ground next to my discarded clothes. Addie is in a lacy bra and matching thong. My mouth goes dry. I run a hand over my jaw as I stare at her, my gaze taking in every inch of her body that I've been forcing myself not to see for days, if not years.

"Fuck, Addie. You're so fucking gorgeous." I slip

one bra strap down her shoulder before I unhook it in the back with one hand and let it fall to her lap.

Full breasts spill out, soft and pale with rosy nipples. I can't stop myself. I lower my head to her chest and kiss the side of her breast, then pull her nipple into my mouth and suck.

"Oh God," Addie groans, her head falling back.

I switch to the other side. Her pulse is hammering in her neck, and knowing I'm the one that's doing that to her is its own reward.

I pull the abandoned bra off her lap and send it flying to the floor. The bed dips when I climb on, gently pressing her legs apart and kneeling between them. My hands find her breasts again, closing around both. They're the perfect handful in my large palm. I rub my thumbs along the sides.

I want to spend all night learning every curve of her body.

The soft swell of her stomach. The dip next to her hipbone, by her collarbone. I want to map every inch of her.

She lifts her hips. Like we've choreographed it, I bring my fingers down to hook into the lacy waistband and pull her underwear down, dragging them slowly over her toned legs.

Even my movements—scooting from between her

legs to get them off her feet, tossing them to the floor, and moving back into position between her spread legs —feels effortless, natural. There isn't any of the awkwardness of a usual first time with someone, the where-do-I-put-my-hands or accidental elbowing when you both move in the same direction at the same time. It's like we've been doing this for years.

In my mind, we have, but I never imagined it could be like this.

I push her legs further apart and keep my hands on her inner thighs as I look at the most beautiful sight I've ever seen. Her arousal glistens in the soft light from the TV that plays silently behind us. I press a kiss to her inner thigh, the moan she lets out giving me the push I need to move my kisses further up her leg.

When I land a kiss on her mound, the moans get louder. She's completely bare and must have waxed because there's no hint of stubble. Just soft, slick skin. I dip my tongue between her folds, just above her clit.

Addie presses her hips up into me, forcing my tongue to press harder against her. I grip her hips with my hands and push her into the bed.

"My turn, baby. Patience," I murmur against her sex.

She just groans in response, a symphony of euphoric noises as I hold her hips in place, giving her what she wants. I swipe my tongue all along her slit in one long, languid motion.

If I thought I loved the taste of her mouth, this is even more addicting. I could bury my face between her thighs for hours.

I give her one more soft pass of my tongue between her legs before I lift myself up and look her in the eye as I bring my hands closer together until my thumbs rub against her pussy lips.

I run my fingers between her legs. "Fuck, Addie. You're soaked." I want to bury myself in her, but I settle for pressing my cock along her slit, teasing her.

"Cam. Please," Addie whimpers, her gaze fixed on mine.

I know what she's asking, but I need to be sure. Not just because of who she is. But because for the first time in my life, I care more about her needs than mine. I can wait. I'll wait forever if I have to, I realize. I'll do whatever Addie needs.

"What do you need, baby?" I ask, my cock pressed against her.

"I want to feel you inside me, Cam," she says, breathless. "I want all of you."

I'm so ready to sink into her, to fill her up, to make her scream, but something stops me. "Shit. I don't have a condom." I pull away from her. My dick protests by getting even harder, if that were even possible.

Addie shakes her head. "It's okay."

"Addie, I—"

"Really," she insists. "I have an IUD. And... I trust you." Her voice softens.

"Are you sure?" I ask, furrowing my brows. I'm clean, of course. I got tested again after things ended with Ellie. But this is up to Addie.

She nods. "I trust you," she says again.

I notch myself at her entrance, the head of my cock just barely pressing inside. She's so hot and wet and ready that it takes all of my control not to drive right into her.

19

ADDISON

Forget the emails that are sitting unanswered in my inbox. Forget everything that's waiting for me back at home, the fact that my makeup and clothes and hair stuff is miles and miles away and I won't be getting any of it back. Forget all the people waiting in line who need something from me.

The only thing I can focus on—the only thing that matters—is Cam between my legs.

He's bigger than I expected, even after seeing the bulge in his boxers. It's heavy between his legs, and pressed against me like this, it seems even larger.

I tilt my hips, needing him inside me, but he holds still. Even as he's asking me what I want, if this is okay, if I'm ready, he's always been the one in control here, and it's driving me crazy.

"Are you ready, Addie?" Cam asks. His voice is strained. I can tell it's taking everything in him to hold himself still right now, and a swell of pride rises inside me. *I did that.*

"Fuck me, Cam. I need you," I pant.

He shakes his head. "This isn't a quick fuck, Addie. There's no coming back from this. If we do this, you're mine."

My heart swells. *This is real.* Holy shit, this is actually happening.

"I'm already yours," I whisper. The words end on a sharp intake of breath as he finally, blissfully, pushes into me.

His cock stretches me, filling me completely. The initial sting fades to warmth as my body adjusts, and he starts to move. Slowly pulling completely out of me before pressing back in. My head drops back against the pillows.

I've never felt this full before, but it's not just physical. It's *everything.*

Cam's head dips to kiss my neck. He's balanced above me, his biceps straining. I put one arm around his neck, holding him to me.

"Are you okay?" he asks, staring into my eyes. "I don't want to hurt your arm."

"I'm good. So good," I manage to moan out. And it is. *So* fucking good. I'm not a virgin, not even close, and at twenty-seven I've dated my fair share of guys. But none of them has ever been like this, so all-consuming. So gentle and so dominant at the same time.

"When your arm is better, I'm going to take you from behind," he grunts, slamming into me so hard I let out a cry. "I want to stare at that gorgeous ass while I'm deep inside you."

"Planning ahead?" My sarcastic tone is lost in my gasp.

Cam stills, his cock deep inside me. His groin presses up against mine, and I can feel his length throbbing inside me. He stares into my eyes. "Yeah, baby. I'm planning ahead. I'm not doing this just once. Mine, remember?" He punctuates his words with another hard thrust, ripping a whine from my throat.

"Oh God, Cam." A low moan follows my words as my body tenses.

"That's right, baby. Come for me."

Because of his touch or his words or both, I unravel, my body tightening, flying higher and higher, and when he says it again—*come for me*—I do, shattering around him as he kisses me hard on the mouth.

He's moving slowly inside me when I come down from my climax, still hard.

"God, Addie. That was gorgeous." He picks up the pace, his chest rapidly rising and falling. "I'm not going to last, baby. Give me another one."

I'm about to open my mouth to tell him I can't, that I've never had more than one, but he brings his hand between us and circles my clit with his thumb, slowly at first, then faster and harder, and I see stars.

"Cam," is all I can manage as a second orgasm starts building, taking over my body as he thrusts hard and deep.

He brings his arms around me, gripping my ass as he pulls me closer to bottom out inside me. We climax together, his hot seed spilling into me while I clench around him. Fuck.

He's breathing hard when he pulls out. I wince at the soreness left over from the way his body stretched mine.

"Stay there, Addie. I'll be right back." Cam slides his boxers on as he walks to the bathroom. When he returns a minute later, he has a washcloth in his hand that he uses to clean me gently.

My eyes are heavy. I put my head on the pillow to

rest for just a minute while Cam goes back into the bathroom, but the next thing I know he's pulling sheets up over me.

"Do you need anything?" he whispers.

I shake my head into the pillow, unable to force my eyes open. Just sleep. That's all I need.

"Can I..." Cam trails off, or maybe I fall asleep while he's talking. "Do you want me to sleep in the other bed?"

I shake my head into the pillow again.

"Addie, I need a real answer, babe. I don't want you to freak out when you wake up next to me."

I manage to blink my eyes open. Cam looks nervous, almost. I'm not sure I've ever seen that expression on him before, and it's endearing. "I want you to sleep with me," I whisper.

A smile spreads across his face. "Good."

He disappears from view as he walks around the bed, and the mattress dips when he climbs in beside me. He moves across the bed until his front is pressed to my back, and he puts an arm around me.

"Does this hurt your arm?" he asks.

"No," I say, relaxing into him. "This is good." The last thing I'm aware of is him kissing the top of my head.

Something hard is pressed up against my back. I wiggle my butt into it for half a second before I realize just what it is and freeze.

"You can keep doing that," Cam mumbles. His voice is thick with sleep, but I can practically hear his smile.

I scoot forward, but the arm around me tightens, holding me against him.

"Five move minutes," he says into my hair.

"Cam," I retort with another wiggle of protest, "I have to get up."

"No." His words are muffled.

"I get that you're not a morning person, but I kind of have to pee." So much for romance.

His grip loosens. I slide out of the bed, stepping over our discarded clothing as I make my way to the bathroom.

As I sit on the toilet, something occurs to me. I don't have any other clothes. I can re-wear the old ones I guess, but I don't think my underwear is going to be clean enough for that. By the time Cam peeled them off me, they were soaked.

I grin to myself. Holy fuck. I slept with Camden Allen.

All those years of pining away finally amounted to something.

But then my grin fades a little.

I slept with Camden Allen. How am I going to tell my brother about this? *Should* I tell my brother? It's not like he knows about everyone I've slept with. If anything, he thinks I'm still a sweet, innocent virgin.

But if Cam and I are dating, it's going to come up.

Holy shit. *Are* we dating? Where do we go from here? He's in the bed wearing nothing but boxers and sporting a hard-on that I'll chalk up to morning wood, and I'm naked in the bathroom with nothing to wear.

This is the kind of situation where, if this were a one-time thing, I'd just hide out in here until he left.

I flush and wash my hands, staring at myself in the mirror. The bruises from my fall are more pronounced now along my arm and side, and I glance down to find more along my leg. They're deep purple. I'm lucky I didn't get more hurt than I did.

I pull a towel from the pile and wrap it around myself as I study my reflection. I'm a hot mess. Red lines and superficial scrapes from my fall crisscross my legs and my arm below the bandage. My hair isn't that nicely mussed post-sex hair. It looks like I stuck my finger in a light socket.

There's a smudge of dirt on one shoulder. My lips

twist into a grimace. God, I can't believe I fell asleep like this last night.

I need a shower. But that brings up a whole host of other issues. What do I do with the stitches? I think they said to keep them dry for twenty-four hours.

I guess I can lean my head back into the water, but it's going to be hard to wash with one hand while keeping the opposite shoulder dry. And how am I going to get the tangles out of my mass of hair? What do I put on afterwards, since all I have are yesterday's clothes, covered in dirt from my fall?

And unrelated but still critical, where's the coffee?

I poke my head into the bedroom. Cam is still sprawled across the bed, and since I moved, he's flopped over onto his stomach. Is that uncomfortable with morning wood? Does that mean it went away, or is it squished into the mattress?

So many questions.

There's a coffee maker on a little tray next to the TV screen. I zero in on it and do my best to be quiet while I tiptoe over and make coffee from a pod provided by the hotel. It's bitter, but it's caffeinated, so we'll take it.

I sit with my coffee by the window. It looks out over the hotel pool, which is empty right now. There are lounge chairs dotting the deck and a bar that I can see from here.

It occurs to me that I don't have a bathing suit, either. I tug on my hair while I swallow another mouthful of the bitter morning brew. We might need to go shopping when Cam wakes up. I start to make a list in my head.

"Hmph." A noise comes from the direction of the bed. As I look over, Cam lifts his head from the pillow and looks around, bleary-eyed. "Is it morning?" he mumbles.

I hide my grin. "It's like nine-thirty. It's been morning for a while."

"Coffee," he says, head falling back to the pillow with a dull *thump*.

I stick another pod into the coffee maker and wait for it to brew. "Are you awake enough to talk?" I ask.

No answer, which I suppose is an answer in itself.

I bring the hot coffee to the bed and sit on the edge with it in my hands. Cam rolls toward me and sits up enough to take a sip, then another before he finally looks up at me.

"What did you want to talk about?"

Ah. So, he's capable of hearing, just not responding before coffee. "We have the day in Nassau. And..." I look at the clothing on the ground. "I need some clothes. And a bathing suit if we want to go to the beach or the pool."

Cam drains the last of his coffee. How does he drink it so fast without burning his throat? "There was a gift shop on the first floor. Can you wear your dirty clothes just to go down there?"

I nod. "But I need, um... underwear." My cheeks heat. I can't believe *this* is what I'm embarrassed about. I had sex with Cam last night. I told him I had to pee. We've been sharing a bathroom for days, and he's had to help me change my shirt. But talking about underwear is apparently where the line is for me.

"You don't need to wear underwear." Cam winks.

I hit him with my good arm.

He winces. "Ow! I'm just saying. I'm in favor of you going commando."

I giggle. "How is that any better?"

He shrugs, a smirk on his lips. "It's not. It's all selfish, unless you count easy access as being a plus for you, too."

I tug on a strand of hair. We should probably talk about this, right? Do I bring it up? Do I wait for him to bring it up?

I'm never one to push or to even be the one who sets boundaries. I tend to go with the flow, say yes to everyone who needs me. And that goes for relationships, too. But with Cam, I feel like I'm floundering. Like he's looking to me for answers, to set the pace here, and I'm scared.

Because what if I get it wrong? Being with him is so comfortable and natural, and I'm afraid I'm going to mess it up.

Cam takes my hand, unwinding the hair from my finger, and holds it tight, our fingers laced together. "Hand me my pants. We're going to head to the gift shop first and find some clothes to wear, and then once we change, we're going to get some breakfast. And you can ask me all those questions that are spiraling in your head."

My eyes must be wide when I look at him, because he just laughs.

"Yeah, you're about as easy to read as a billboard, Addie. Stop freaking out. We'll talk about everything you want to know, but if we sit in bed too much longer, I'm going to pull you down and fuck you again, so get your hot little ass moving."

20

CAM

"How about this one?" Addie asks, holding up a piece of fabric that I think is meant to be a bikini.

I tilt my head. "Where's the rest of it?"

She squints at it. "This is all of it. It's a bathing suit."

"It looks like underwear." Teasing aside, I'm practically drooling at the thought of seeing her in that.

She lifts her chin defiantly. "I'm getting it."

I snatch it from her hand.

"Hey! I said I'm getting that," she says, stomping her foot.

I wrap an arm around her and pull her close to speak right in her ear. "I'm buying it for you. Go find whatever else you need. And don't stamp your foot or I'll spank that hot little ass."

She gives a little squeal and heads off to browse through more racks, and I watch as she goes. Even in day-old shorts and un-showered, she's gorgeous.

The gift shop is pretty well-stocked. We were able to find a hairbrush, bathing suits for both of us, two extra t-shirts each, and a skirt for Addie. They even had underwear, although Addie wrinkled her nose at the simple cotton briefs.

I watch her flit around the store. She's exactly the same Addie I've known for so long, and somehow the way I see her has completely changed since last night. Before last night, if I'm honest. I don't know when I went from seeing her as Maddox's little sister to a woman, but she's firmly fixed in my mind in her new role. And ideally in a role as my girlfriend, if I have my way.

I thought I was over relationships, but it's different with Addie somehow. With her, it's... easy. I don't have to work constantly at it.

I know she's a people-pleaser, though. She has trouble saying no. I've seen it over and over again when I'm with her family. And there's nothing wrong with giving in when your family wants you to be the Christmas Elf during the holidays.

But with us, she's going to be the one to set the boundaries. I'm not going to be another person that she has to try to make happy. It's all up to her and on her timeline.

I set our haul on the counter and dig out a credit card. We're going to have to tell Maddox. He can't be mad, though. Right? I'm a nice guy. I'll treat Addie right, and I'm not in this for a quick fuck. I meant what I said last night. Once we took that step, I was ready to place my bets and let it ride. I'm not pulling out of this unless it's what she wants.

The cashier hands my card back and starts to stick our purchases in a bag when Addie walks up holding a pair of flip-flops. "Can I add these?" She flashes puppy dog eyes.

I shrug to the cashier and pull my card out again. While he runs it, I turn to Addie. "Do you want to eat here after we change? Or do you want to find a restaurant?"

"What do you want to do?"

I shake my head, smiling. "I'm not deciding this one. It's up to you."

She taps a finger on her chin while she thinks for a little too long, probably trying to figure out what I really want and choose that. "Maybe breakfast here, and then we can go out for lunch? I want more of those conch fritters."

"Excellent choice," I say, nodding. It's exactly what I would have chosen myself.

We bring our bag back upstairs, and I take the tags off the clothing while Addie goes into the bathroom to wash her hair. She was instructed to keep the bandage on her arm dry, so I can't imagine it'll be easy. I set the hairbrush on the counter and turn to see Addie staring at the shower like it's a complex math equation she needs to solve.

"Do you need help?"

She shakes her head, too quickly. "I can do it."

"I know you can. I'm just offering to help, since you only have one good arm right now. It's okay to need help. I'm happy to do it," I assure her.

I realize that part didn't occur to her. She'd been working out how to keep the bandage dry, but even I use two hands to wash my hair.

She hesitates. "It wouldn't be—"

"Weird? Stop asking that, Addie. Nothing is weird with us. You need help, and I'm here for you. I'm sure if I needed help with something you'd offer, right?"

"Yeah," she says, tugging on a lock of hair.

"So just remember this next time I ask you for

something. Take your clothes off and I'll help you wash your hair."

Her eyes widen, and I raise my eyebrows. "Addie, I've seen you naked. Did you forget everything about last night already?"

Her cheeks color. "No..."

"And I'm going to see you naked again—plenty of times, if I have anything to say about it. Take the shorts off, and I'll help you with your shirt."

It takes an entire bottle of hotel shampoo to wash her long hair. "Don't forget conditioner," she says, her eyes closed as I rinse her red locks, and I don't miss that she asked for something she needs. We're making progress.

I look at the options lined up on the shelf. Body wash, lotion... conditioner. Got it. I smear it on her hair and rinse again. Magically, it transforms her hair into a shiny, smooth wave. So that's what it does.

"Okay, Addie. All set," I say, taking a step back. I pluck a towel off the rack and hold it up, wrapping it around her body as she eases out. "Do you need any more help?"

She does some maneuver to the towel that keeps it tight around her chest, even when she takes her hands away. "I think I'm good. Maybe just some help to brush my hair or something. It's kind of hard to do with one hand. I'll dry off and get dressed first, though."

I leave her alone in the bathroom, wondering how in the hell she plans to fasten a bra with one hand, but somehow she manages to get into her clothes. When the bathroom door opens, she's fully dressed, and a towel is wrapped around her head like a turban.

"Do you want help brushing your hair?" I ask.

She chews her lip for a minute before she nods and grabs the brush from the bathroom. "Start at the bottom and work your way up."

It takes a solid ten minutes, but Addie's hair is free of tangles by the time she goes to dry it—another ten minutes—and then we're headed out the door.

Breakfast in the hotel rivals most restaurants back home. We load our plates with grits, some kind of meat that goes on top, Johnny cakes, and conch chowder. Addie grabs an extra plate just for fruit.

"I don't know if I want to go put on a bikini," she says as she takes the last bite of her grits, patting her stomach where it's pooched out the tiniest bit. "I have a food baby."

"It's hot. I love your food baby," I reassure her. "Do you want to do something else first? We can hang around the island and then go to the pool later on. After you digest, if you want."

She giggles. "I think I'm going to have another food baby after lunch, but yeah. I'm already dressed in clean clothes. We may as well check out whatever else is on the island."

A stack of brochures by the front desk offers suggestions for things to do. Snorkeling, a glass-bottom boat tour... ATV tours.

"Want to try ATVs again?" Addie says, a teasing note in her voice.

I wince. "Too soon." I pluck the brochure from her hand and bury it under the others. "How about this?"

She takes the glossy paper from my hand. "Swim with pigs? Um, hard pass. If I'm not supposed to get stitches wet, I'm pretty sure they'd frown on exposing the cut to pigs."

"Good point." I leaf through the remaining brochures.

Addie chews on her lower lip. "This might be boring, but what about just walking? Like along the beach, or around the island? I've never been here before this trip, so it would be fun to see more of it."

Anything with Addie is fun, if you ask me. I'm

never bored when I'm around her. "I love that idea. Let's go."

Just off the main island is a smaller one called Paradise Island. The two are connected by a bridge. We take a cab, spending the entire ride with our faces close to the windows like a couple of kids watching the view.

"Are those the pigs people pay to swim with? Out there in the bay?" Addie asks, pointing.

I follow her gaze. "Looks like it. Apparently, it's a big thing."

The cab driver grunts. "Good for tourists, those pigs."

Addie covers her mouth to hold back her giggles.

The cab drops us off near the beach. I take Addie's hand as we make our way down to the shore and slip off our shoes. We hold them in our hands as we walk along the waterline. My toes curl into the warm sand while the waves lap gently against our feet.

"God, this place," Addie sighs, looking out over the blue water that spans endlessly toward the horizon. "It's just gorgeous. I wonder what it would be like to live here."

"It would be magical," I murmur, following her

gaze. "Imagine listening to the sound of the waves every day."

Addie stops and picks up a spiral seashell, brushing off the sand to admire it. "I guess it's also that we're on vacation right now, huh? Like, anywhere you don't have to get up in the morning to go to work probably feels relaxing."

"True. Vacation goggles." I nod.

She giggles. "Exactly." Addie looks at me, squinting against the late morning sun. "What would you do if you ever decided to stop playing poker? Or do you think you'll keep doing that forever?"

It's a subject I've thought a lot about lately. "I've always wanted to teach. I majored in applied math and education in college and kind of figured that I'd use that, but I never did."

Addie's eyes widen. "How did I never know that?"

"I'm guessing it's because if you heard Maddox and I talking back then, the logical assumption would be that we were majoring in beer pong. We didn't talk much about academics."

She nods slowly, thinking as she watches a boat on the horizon. "Makes sense. I don't know that I talked a lot about my studies during my time off, either." Addie turns and looks at me. "Did you plan on teaching? What were you going to do with your degree?"

We take a few more steps along the water. "Originally, I was actually planning to get a doctorate so I could be a college professor. I kind of figured that's the age group I'm best suited for, you know? But then I got started in poker, and it just seemed like so much to go back to school, you know? And especially now, seeing Blake all stressed with his post-doc stuff, I'm not sure that's the lifestyle I want. So... maybe high school? Middle school at the very youngest. I'm not sure I know much about kids."

Addie laughs. "Just hang out with Julio for a while. He'll get you up to speed."

21

ADDISON

ANNIKA

You didn't say yes to the senior class advisor thing, did you? She's emailing all of us. Don't cave.

Remember, No is a complete sentence, Addie.

Not yet. Thinking about it, though.

Addie! How in the hell are you going to have time for that?

You can't just give in to everything people want all the time.

shrug emoji It'll be fine. And if it doesn't work out or it's a huge pain, I'll quit. Probably.

Don't kill yourself just so other people will be happy.

Speaking of making people happy...

Yes? *eyeballs emoji*

So the guy. The one I had a crush on.

???

He's not just a crush anymore.

!!!

Details please!

Insanely long story. But our day in the Bahamas we went ATVing and I crashed.

WTF Addie? Are you okay?

Yeah, I'm fine. But I ended up having to get stitches, so we were stuck at the hospital, and we missed the boat.

Oh shit.

Yeah. So we're stuck in the Bahamas. At least I brought my phone. Cam left his on the ship. And we have our passports. Turns out there's a reason they tell you to take it with you when you leave the ship.

So how are you getting back?

We have a flight home tomorrow. Cam is with me.

Oooh, a mini honeymoon already!

Well... maybe a little. We're staying in a hotel room together.

Oh, I'm gonna need so many more details when you get home girl.

Just wanted to let you know some of the drama. But I'm safe, and I'll be back in Philly tomorrow.

I'm staying over at your place tomorrow night. Lots to talk about.

So many details already. I'll let you know how tonight goes... *wink emoji*

Cam and I have lunch on Paradise island— more conch fritters and more conversation. This island is smaller than the main one, and everything seems slower here, more peaceful. Or maybe it's Cam that has me feeling this way. He's so easy to talk to. We talk about friends, family, what's on our bucket list.

I can't help but be surprised by the last item on Cam's list.

"I want to settle down. Get married, have a family," he admits, then pops another bite of Johnny cake into his mouth.

I mean, same. But are you supposed to say that to the guy you're dating? *Are* we dating?

"I want to go skydiving," I blurt out, then stuff a fritter in my mouth.

Cam tilts his head, smiling like he knows exactly what's on my mind. "You don't want to get married?"

Do I tell him I spent most of ninth grade doodling *Mrs. Camden Allen* and *Addison Allen* on my notebooks?

"Uh, someday," I hedge, swallowing over the lump in my throat.

"Well, I'm at a point in my life where I'm not going to start a relationship with someone if I don't see it at least having potential to go that direction." Cam puts his fork down and looks at me intently.

My mouth goes dry, and I grab my water and take a few gulps.

Does that mean he sees that with me? Are we really in a relationship? Shit. Be a grown-up, Addie. He's been inside you. Plus, it's Cam. You can ask him anything.

I set the glass down harder than I intend to. "Are we starting a relationship, Cam?" I look him in the eye.

"There she is," he says, a smirk growing on his face.

My eyes narrow. "What does that mean?"

Cam reaches across the table and covers my hand with his. "I don't want you to be different around me now, Addie. You've never been one to be shy or hold things back. You've always just said what's on your mind. I like that about you. So, to answer your question, yes, I want to start a relationship with you. Does that answer those questions that have been floating around in your mind?"

"You want another virgin piña colada?" I ask Cam, swinging my legs to the side of the lounge chair. "I'm going to get another daquiri."

He nods. "Charge it to the room, okay?"

I can feel his eyes on me as I walk toward the poolside bar. This bathing suit might be even better than the little white one I left on the ship. It hugs my curves in just the right way. When I put it on, Cam's eyes darkened with lust, and I had to practically drag him out of our room to come to the pool.

After lunch, we came back to the hotel, and we've been lounging on chairs in the sun while I reapply sunscreen every ten minutes or so. The poolside bar makes amazing drinks that we've been sipping on while we eat our way through their snack menu. It's so relaxing that I think I might like it even better than sightseeing. My arm is already feeling better, and I can feel the throbbing pain slowly subsiding as we sit in the sun. The doctors told me it needed to stay totally dry for twenty-four hours, but we're getting close to that.

I use my phone to look up "Can you swim with stitches?" and find plenty of warnings against swimming in potentially bacteria-laden areas. I peer at the pool. It looks clean, but there are a lot of people here. And little kids. I've been around enough of them to know at least two of those kids have likely peed in the pool already today. I pout a little.

"What's wrong?" Cam asks, looking over at me

from where he's sipping a virgin piña colada on a lounge chair.

It appears to be his drink of choice when he has something other than soda. I think he's had three of them today. I made fun of his girly drink the first time he ordered it, but the teasing has lost its novelty, because Cam truly doesn't care. He just likes his little drink with the umbrella and cherries.

"I want to go swimming," I whine, leaning to my side to look at Cam.

"And? Are you supposed to do that with stitches?" His forehead wrinkles as he thinks.

I was hoping he'd tell me it was fine, negating what I've seen online. Cam telling me what I want to hear is obviously better advice than whatever physician wrote this website. I hold up my phone, the results of the internet search still showing on the screen.

"Apparently not in dirty things like pools. But I was hoping they were just being overdramatic," I admit, my mood souring a pinch.

He leans back against the headrest and closes his eyes. "Huh. Whatever would we do without phones to look everything up?"

We'd be able to go swimming, that's what.

Cam's response was almost sarcastic, and I know he left his phone behind when we left the ship, but his comment makes me realize I haven't seen him with a phone in... a long time. I furrow my brows as I think. It's been since we boarded the ship, in fact.

"I haven't even seen you check your phone. I'm glued to mine even on vacation. How can you keep yourself from checking it? The emails would pile up if I didn't go through them every day."

He doesn't open his eyes, but one side of his lips curves in a smile. "I left it in my duffel bag for the trip, turned off. It's been peaceful. At least as far as texts and phone calls are concerned."

Peace and quiet sound good, but... "What are you going to do about a phone? Are you just going to wait until they mail your stuff back?"

"Nah. I'm due for an upgrade anyway. I'll get a new one and mail back the old one as a trade-in once I get it back." He winks at me. "Maybe I can even call you with my fancy new phone. It gets lonely at poker tournaments, you know. I might need a video call to see a friendly face. Or... something."

My face heats as butterflies swarm in my stomach at the idea of *that* kind of call.

I cover my mouth as I let out a loud yawn.

We've just finished dinner and I'm starting to get sleepy, between the sun and the cocktails and the glass of wine I had with my meal. We'd talked earlier about exploring the island at night, but I'm not sure I have the energy.

"Let's just get you to bed," Cam says with a soft smile. His hand is on my elbow as I stand from my chair, and once I'm steady, he slides it down to hold my hand.

His hand is perfect—not too big, not too small. Warm and comforting instead of being clammy or sweaty. And he holds my hand with the perfect grip strength. It makes me feel safe, the way he takes charge when I need him to and the way he takes care of me.

And it's making me think about last night. I've had sex before obviously, despite what my brother would probably like to think. I'm twenty-seven. I lost my virginity freshman year of college, and since then, I've dated a handful of guys.

I'm not ashamed to say I like sex. And with the right partner, it can be amazing. I thought I'd had mind-blowing sex with some of my ex-boyfriends.

But all of that pales in comparison to what I felt last night with Cam. I'm not talking about just his size, although that's... shall we say, a *large* factor. He fit with me perfectly. It was like we were made for each other.

It's how our bodies felt so in *sync*. How he knew what I needed without me asking. Maybe it's because we've known one another so long, but part of me wonders if it's something else between us. If that's the reason sex with him was so far beyond anything I'd ever experienced.

Was it just because it was our first time after so much buildup and sexual tension between us? There's only one way to really find out. And we've already established that Cam and I will be sharing a bed tonight.

Suddenly, I'm not so tired.

Cam unlocks the door to our room, my hand still held firmly in his. He holds the door and lets me go so I can walk through before he follows me in and locks the door behind us.

Then I'm the one who takes his hand, leading him to the center of the room, between the two beds.

I keep my gaze locked on Cam's face as I sink to my knees in front of him. His eyes widen, and his pupils dilate with lust.

"Addie, you don't have to—"

"I want to make you feel good," I whisper. "Let me do this for you, Cam."

He doesn't protest as I unbutton his jeans and push them down, then drag his boxers down to join them. His cock is long and hard, with a drop of precum already glistening at the tip. I dart my tongue out to taste it.

Cam lets out a groan. "Fuck, Addie."

I take that as encouragement to run my tongue along his entire length, from the tip down to the base and back up, before I take him into my mouth. He's big, and by the time I fit most of him in my mouth, he's hitting the back of my throat.

"So fucking good, Addie," he says, his voice strained.

I moan and watch his eyes roll back from the vibrations.

"Get on the bed," he grits out.

I shake my head. I want to do this to him, want to watch him lose his mind because of me.

Cam fists my ponytail and pulls me off his cock. "Get on the bed, Addie. If I come, it's going to be inside you."

22

CAM

Addie lets out a little whine, but she sheds her clothes and climbs onto the bed. I'm so hard it borders on painful. She leans against the pillows, but I shake my head.

"You wanted to control this one. You're going to ride me." I settle myself against the pillows and guide her hips, moving her into place as she positions herself over me.

Addie sinks down onto my cock in one smooth movement. Her warmth grips me like a glove. We fit together so perfectly. As our eyes meet, something shifts inside me. Like I told Addie last night, she's mine now. But it's more than that. This is the start of something big.

I groan her name as she starts to move. "So good, Addie. You were fucking made for me, baby."

She throws her head back, giving me a perfect view of her neck and collarbone. I want to sink my teeth into that angle between her shoulder and her neck. I want to kiss along her collarbone, to run my fingers through her hair. I could spend the rest of my life exploring Addison's body and it still wouldn't be enough time.

She's slick with arousal, and even as tight as she is, we move effortlessly together. She rolls her hips, taking me deeper and making me see stars.

"Oh God, Cam," she says on a gasp, her pussy tightening around me. "I'm close."

I hold onto her hips while she moves. This is our last night in the Bahamas before we go back to reality, and I don't know what things are going to look like for us once we're there. But it feels like we're just at the beginning of something big.

My sheets are moving.

I pull them tighter against me, but it just makes the wiggling worse. What the hell kind of dream is this?

A muffled voice comes from somewhere near me. "Cam! Let me go!"

"Need the sheets to sleep," I mutter, trying to slide back into the peaceful slumber I was enjoying.

"Cam!"

I yelp as something hard connects with my shin, making me drop my grip on the sheets altogether. They pull away from me as Addie stands up and wraps herself in one of them, leaving me stark naked and very much awake on the mattress.

"You are the worst morning person ever," she grumbles, taking my sheets with her as she heads toward the coffee pot.

I drowsily rub my eyes. "Why did you kick me?"

"So you'd let me go. I need coffee." Addie isn't much of a morning person today, either.

"Why are you awake?"

"Flight home." She presses the button, and the noise of the brewing coffee pot fills the room.

I place a pillow over my lap as I sit up and reach for the coffee Addie hands me. We sit together in silence with the steaming paper cups.

"Do you need to take a shower?" I manage to form a complete sentence once I finish my first cup and the caffeine starts to hit my bloodstream.

Addie shakes her head. "I'm good. I'm just going

to put my hair up for the plane ride." She takes the last sip. "More coffee?" She gestures with the cup.

I hand her my now very empty one. "Always."

I watch her walk across the room, still wrapped in the sheet. Is there anything sexier than a woman with hair mussed by sex, that pink tinge to her cheeks, and knowing that you're the one that got her there?

I feel a strange sense of pride, and at the same time, longing. I need her again.

Addie turns around, a full cup of coffee in hand. "Oh, no you don't."

"What?" I ask innocently.

She comes back to stand next to the bed but holds the cup just out of my reach. "We don't have time to have sex again. We'll miss our flight. And our track record for getting places on time is not great this vacation." She drops her voice to a whisper. "But if you want to join the mile high club, I might be up for that."

That wakes me right up. Talk about good motivation. "Fine. Give me the coffee and I'll get up."

She smirks. "It'll be in the bathroom. Time to get out of bed, sunshine."

There are two types of people.

The kind that get to the airport two hours early to check in and get through security, even when you're not checking bags, and the kind that don't want to wait at the gate and figure that getting there just before they close the plane doors is bordering on too early.

I'm a generally laid-back guy, but airport schedules aren't known for being flexible. I like to get there ahead of time, relax in the airport, maybe get an overpriced snack while I wait.

Addie is looking at me like I'm crazy, though, now that we're standing in front of the departures board and she realizes when our plane is scheduled to take off. "Our flight isn't for another two *hours*?" she says, incredulous.

"An hour and forty minutes." Perfect timing, if you ask me.

We got here just before noon. I've known Addie long enough to know she's a last-minute kind of flier, so I told her our flight was at noon. There's no way we would have made it on time if I'd told her we were really leaving at two. We'd be standing here at 1:55 on the dot.

"What the hell do we do for that long?" she sputters.

I nudge her with my hip. "We relax. Drink coffee.

Or wine, if you want. Have lunch. Go to the bookstore or something. Whatever we want."

Addie rolls her eyes at me. "I knew I should have double checked what time we had to leave."

"You would have had us rushing and stressed. This way is better, trust me." I sling an arm over her shoulder as we walk down the hallway of the terminal, and toward the food court.

Addie perks up once she realizes there are conch fritters available here. We snack on the fried seafood while Addie has a glass of wine and I have a Coke. It's barely past noon, but time doesn't seem to matter when you're in an airport.

There's still an hour until our flight after we finish eating. We peruse a bookstore, where I pick up a new mystery and Addie gets a book of crosswords, along with a pen.

I look at the cover as I pay for our purchases. Extra challenging? And a pen, not a pencil. Every day I learn something new about Addie, and it makes me like her even more. God knows I'd never be able to finish one of these crosswords. Sudoku I can do. Word games, not so much.

We pick two seats by our gate. Addie pulls out her crosswords and goes to work, the tip of her tongue sticking out the side of her mouth adorably as she works.

I try to focus on my book, but every few minutes I look over at Addie, who's engrossed in the puzzle. She manages to finish one puzzle entirely and is starting on another when they start to board the plane.

I elbow her gently. "Addie, we're boarding."

Her head pops up. "Huh?"

I nod toward the gate. "They're boarding first class. That's us."

She shoves the crosswords into her backpack which holds the few possessions we have with us and stands to board the plane.

I've flown first class, but only once, for a friend's bachelor party in Vegas. But all the flying to tournaments adds up, and I was able to upgrade us with miles. I forgot how nice it is. It's almost worth paying for. Addie and I settle into the seats, enjoying the extra space. A flight attendant offers us drinks before takeoff.

"This is amazing," Addie whispers to me, sipping on her soda. "I don't know if I want to go back to flying in the cheap seats after this. When do we get to join the Mile High Club?"

"Totally worth it," I sigh, leaning against the head rest as I wait for takeoff and doing my best to look relaxed, even though I'm pretty sure Addie can tell that my entire body is tight with the anticipation of joining the Mile High Club with her. "And once we're actually a mile high. It doesn't count if we're still on the runway."

An hour into the flight, Addie leans over. "I'm going to the bathroom."

I lift an eyebrow. "Yeah?"

She wiggles her own eyebrows at me. "I'll be waiting." She unbuckles her seatbelt and heads for the front of the plane.

This is the dream, right? Flying first class with a girl who wants to join the Mile High Club. I mentally high five teenage Cam. If only that pimply, scrawny kid could see me now.

I give it a couple of minutes, then make my way toward the bathroom and knock gently. The door cracks open. I squeeze in, and immediately I realize why this is a fantasy, not reality.

There's barely enough room in here for one person.

But this was Addie's idea, and if this is what she wants, I'm going to make it happen.

Addie shimmies her hips as she takes her pants

down. I fumble with my belt buckle, my elbow smacking the door. *Smooth, Cam.*

I size up the situation. There's not much room here, and I don't have much faith in the door to support me fucking Addie up against it, let alone how loud that would probably be. So maybe... "Turn around," I whisper.

She does, putting her back to my front—and almost falling into the toilet.

"Shit!" she whispers loudly as she closes the lid.

I work my pants down awkwardly. Teenage Cam would never forgive me if I had the opportunity to join the Mile High Club and let it pass by. We're doing this. No matter how ungraceful this may be.

And it's *really* fucking ungraceful.

"Take your underwear off," I whisper to Addie. I run my hand over her ass as she pulls them down. I'm starting to think that maybe this could work when an elbow catches me in the gut.

"Oof," I say, trying to catch my breath.

"Crap. Sorry," she says, trying to turn around.

Someone knocks on the door.

"Uh, one minute!" I call. This is not going the way I envisioned.

Addie elbows me again, this time missing my balls by a mere inch. This is fucking dangerous.

A roar fills the small space, and Addie lets out a little scream, startling me.

"Shit. I hit the flush button," Addie mutters. "Sorry." She looks over her shoulder at me. A smile plays at her lips, and as our eyes meet, we both burst into laughter.

Any chance of us actually joining the Mile High Club is gone now, but this is going to turn into a story we'll laugh at for years. "Remind me why people do this again?"

She's laughing so hard she can barely catch her breath. A little snort escapes, and she slaps a hand over her mouth. "I don't know. It seemed better in my fantasy, honestly. This is really cramped and uncomfortable. Not really romantic."

"You almost got me in the nuts with your elbow. Talk about killing the romance."

We're both laughing uncontrollably as I help her to straighten and we pull our pants back up.

"Can this be like a bucket list thing that we can now say we've done? Technically, we took our pants off, so I think it's close enough," Addie says, trying to wash her hands while I squeeze into the remaining space.

"Hey, this was your idea," I remind her.

She shrugs. "I thought it would be hotter than this."

I laugh again as I kiss her, long and deep. "Now, let's figure out how to get the door open so I can get out. You might have to stand on the toilet."

Addie manages to squeeze into the corner out of the way while I pull the door open and slide out, thanking God that whoever knocked on the door isn't standing there waiting.

The flight attendant is pouring a drink in the galley when I walk by, but she looks up from what she's doing to give me a knowing smile. "Enjoying your flight, sir?"

Addie and I look at one another and dissolve in laughter every time the flight attendant walks by. I'm sure we're not the first couple she's seen hook up in the bathroom, but it feels naughty and risqué and makes us feel like we have a secret, even if we didn't actually have sex.

"We can't tell my brother about that," Addie says at one point, still giggling.

My heart drops, because in our escape from reality

I'd almost forgotten just why we were never supposed to start any of this.

"Um," I say, unsure how to start. "Maybe we shouldn't tell him about any of this. For a little bit, at least."

Addie nods, deep in thought. "I'm not sure he'd be the most accepting of this whole thing. He might skin you alive."

"Yeah. Or worse." I can think of a whole host of things Maddox might do. He's protective of the people he loves, almost to a fault.

"We should probably keep it under wraps until we're sure. Like, no point in stirring the pot if this doesn't work out between us."

I turn in my seat to face her. "Addie." She turns to look at me, and I grip her chin between my thumb and forefinger. "I'm—I know you might need time. But I'm sure here. I know I've said that, but it's—I'm not just saying that. It's true. I wouldn't have started something, wouldn't have slept with you, if I didn't see this going somewhere. I wouldn't do that to you."

She blinks, her eyes searching my face. "I know," she says softly.

"*Please fasten your seat belts and return your seats to their upright position as we prepare for landing,*" the flight attendant announces overhead.

Addie and I follow her instructions, and I wonder if our conversation is over until she reaches over and slides her hand into mine.

She's still holding my hand when we touch down back in reality.

23

ADDISON

To: AAnderson@brynmawrschools.com
From: JosieChrisAndersonFleming@mail.com
Subject: Re: Favor

Thank you so much for being willing to watch the twins! Seriously, you're the best. Maybe like 2 p.m. on Sunday?

Chris

"Oh!" I exclaim as we walk through the airport doors, toward the parking shuttle while I check my email. "I almost forgot. I said I'd watch Josie's twins this Sunday. Want to help?"

"You want me to babysit?" Cam wrinkles his nose.

I smack his arm. "It'll be fun, and it'll be a chance for us to hang out. That's all."

He actually looks like he's considering it. "Are you sure? I'm not sure I know that much about babies. How old are they? Like a month?"

"They're ten months. Not really baby-babies. Almost toddlers. I don't think they're walking yet, but I know they can crawl. It'll be fun." I'm not positive on the fun aspect, but I don't want to do this alone. I know what a handful kids this age can be, and there are two of them. And toddler math isn't like regular math, where one plus one equals two. If you add one toddler plus one toddler, you get about eight times the destruction.

He finally nods. "Sure. Where?"

Relief washes over me. I suppose I could have asked Annika if Cam said no, but he's the one I want to spend time with.

Plus, Annika would probably put the twins in

timeout or ground them or something. She's strict when it comes to her students, and I'm not sure she's any more flexible when it comes to smaller kids.

"They're staying at Maddox's house, dog-sitting. He's on his honeymoon."

"I know," he says, giving me a look that reminds me, once again, that this is my brother's best friend I'm sleeping with. That I have feelings for.

I'm not willing to think about our situation too much right now. I just want to pretend we're still in the Bahamas, sipping cocktails poolside.

As I think about the cocktails, something occurs to me. I had my share of drinks, but I'm not sure I ever saw Cam drink something other than soda. Even the piña coladas he had at the casino he ordered without alcohol.

I rack my brain, thinking back to Maddox's wedding, of all the Thanksgiving and Christmas dinners he's shared with my family. I can't remember ever seeing him drink alcohol.

He never made a big deal of it, so I hadn't actually picked up on it until now.

"Cam?" I say after a moment.

"Hmm?" He looks at me as we climb into the shuttle bus.

I wait until we sit down at the back. "Not that it

matters. But how come you don't drink? Or did I miss something? It just seemed like..."

Cam shakes his head. "You're right. I don't."

He doesn't elaborate, and he sets his mouth in a thin line that indicates he's done talking about it.

"Does it bother you when I do?"

He looks over at me. "No. I don't mind. It's just a personal choice."

I nod silently, waiting for him to decide if he wants to say more about it. But he just reaches over and gives my thigh a gentle squeeze without saying anything else.

We're standing next to Cam's Subaru before it occurs to either of us.

"Shit," he mutters, staring at the locked car.

"The keys are still on the ship, aren't they?" We should have realized this sooner. Maybe we would have, if we hadn't been in a sex haze for the last two days.

He nods with a resigned sigh. "I'll have to grab my extra set. And get the doorman to let me in to my apartment to get those." A frown crosses his face.

I offer him a wry smile. "This whole trip really took a crappy turn, huh?"

His frown disappears as he looks at me. "I think it took a really great one, Addie. I wouldn't change this for the world. The car keys and my phone and all that stuff... it's all replaceable. Time with you isn't."

"Except the sex. There's more where that came from." I give him a wink.

He roars with laughter as he folds me into his arms. "Let's go see if we can solve some of this. Can you get an Uber with your phone?"

I sigh as I close my apartment door and lean my back against it. It's only 8:30, but it feels like midnight after the day we've had, shuttling between the airport, my apartment, Cam's apartment, and back to the airport with the extra keys.

I know Annika wanted to come over for gossip tonight. I'm torn, because I have so much to tell her, and I need her opinion on this whole Cam thing. And in person, not over text messaging. But I'm ready to drop into bed without even brushing my teeth.

I send Annika a text to see what she's doing and if we can move our girl talk to tomorrow night, rubbing a tired hand over my eyes.

ANNIKA

> Just got home, kind of fried but so much to tell you. Gossip tomorrow or do you want to come over here?

> If you were 22, you'd barely be pregaming at this point. Stop being such an old lady. I'm coming over. You want pizza?

> And breadsticks, please.

Annika arrives at my apartment twenty minutes later with a pizza, breadsticks, and a six pack of hard cider. I twist the cap off one of the bottles, thinking of Cam and the first time he's ever dodged a question I asked. What reason for not drinking could be so terrible he doesn't want to tell me?

Annika shoves the pizza box at me. "Okay, girl. Talk. I want to hear everything."

I laugh as I follow her into the kitchen. "Pizza first. I haven't eaten since we got off the plane. It took way too long to get back home from the airport. Long story."

Annika pulls the top off of her bottle of cider and takes a long sip. "Start at the beginning. You showed up on the cruise ship. And?"

I walk the few steps from the kitchen to the living room and sink onto the couch with my cider in one hand and a slice of pizza in the other. "Well, first, Maddox did *not* warn him I was coming. He was completely caught off guard that I was there. And on top of that, we had to share a room."

"The bunk beds," she says, nodding. "I remember. Any college-style antics in the room?"

I shake my head as I swallow my bite of pizza. "No, nothing like that. He actually seemed like he was avoiding me for the first day or so. Then we had a big fight after the bikini thing. But he was, like... calm during it. He just let me get everything off my chest."

She raises her eyebrows. "He didn't get mad?"

"No. He let me rant, then after I shut myself in the bathroom to change, he apologized. And asked if we could be friends."

"Uh-huh. And how did being *friends* work out for you?"

I lean back on the sofa after finishing my slice and wipe my hands on my shorts. "Well, you know some of it. I told you about the ATVs and how I had to get stitches and all of that."

Annika puts her pizza on her lap. "Oh, shit! I forgot about that. How are you?"

"I'm fine. It doesn't really hurt anymore. But it was kind of a pain to have stitches. Besides the fact that we missed getting back on the ship and got stuck in the Bahamas, I had to keep it dry so I couldn't go in the pool."

My cheeks heat, thinking of Cam tenderly washing my hair. Maybe Annika doesn't need to know *everything*.

She gives me a pointed look. "So what else? More details, please."

I shrug, trying to keep my face neutral. I usually tell Annika everything. But some of the details and the things Cam and I shared seem too special. I want to keep them just between Cam and me.

"Okay, fine, keep your secrets. But you did it, right? Please tell me you banged."

Annika is on my left, so I have to reach across myself to smack her with my good hand, almost spilling my half-full bottle of cider in the process. "We're not living in a frat house, Anni. We did not *bang*. We had sex like two consenting adults." I smile. "And it was fucking amazing."

Annika brushes pizza crumbs off her hands and goes to the kitchen, returning with another slice. "So, now what? Are you together? Or was this just a vacation thing?"

I tug on my hair. "I... I want it to be more. And I think he does, too. But we're going to keep it quiet for a little. I mean, he's my brother's best friend. I'm not sure Maddox is going to take it well."

"Makes sense. When are you going to see him again?"

Annika and I talk until neither of us can keep our eyes open. She crashes in her usual spot on the couch, and I flop into bed.

I consider taking a shower before bed, but I realize that my hairbrush, hair dryer, and most of my products are on a ship somewhere. Hopefully they're making their way back to me once Cam gets his new phone and gets in touch with them, but that doesn't help me right now.

I'll have to make a trip to the mall this weekend to replace everything I left behind. At least I had my phone with me when we got stranded, and my wallet. All I have to replace is beauty supplies. My clothes weren't anything irreplaceable, either, although the bikinis were new.

As I drift off to sleep, I'm making a mental list of things to get done before I have to go back to school on Monday.

It feels like I've barely been asleep for a minute or

two when pans clang together in the kitchen. What the hell is Annika doing?

She pushes open my bedroom door, and daylight spills in from the living room.

"Do you have eggs?" Annika asks, talking way too loudly for what seems like a very early morning hour.

"What?" I pull my pillow over my face to block her out. "Why are you awake? Why do you not have coffee in your hand?"

There is no reason to be up early today, so I want to sleep as long as humanly possible.

Annika's footsteps retreat to the kitchen and then return. I'm about to chuck a pillow at her when the smell of coffee rouses me enough to reconsider.

"Give," I demand. That's about the longest sentence I'm capable of this early.

Annika does not, in fact, give. "I'll put it in the bathroom for you."

I want to murder her, but I'd have to get out of bed for that, and if I'm getting up I'm going for the coffee before I turn to crime. It's not lost on me, even in my barely-conscious state, that this is literally *exactly* what I did to Cam yesterday.

Maybe if things work out between us, we can invest in some kind of magic service that brings coffee to you in bed.

Hold on. I'm still half asleep, but not completely. I shouldn't be stuck in a dream world. And that's what it is, right, to imagine Cam and I living together?

Jesus, I need caffeine.

24

CAM

"Take this," Josie says the second the door opens, shoving a baby at me so fast I almost mistake it for a flesh-colored bulldog.

Maybe not the most attractive analogy, but its pudgy face is screwed up in a wail, and it looks about as happy to see me as a guard dog.

I'm already regretting this decision as Josie disappears through the front door in a sweep of black, shiny hair.

But Addie is also being saddled with a child, although hers isn't screaming just yet. Its frown is one of suspicion. Clearly, the more intelligent of the twins. The one I'm holding seems to be well aware he's being left in the care of two people who don't know the first thing about babies.

At least, I don't. I'm hoping Addie knows something, or this is going to be a really, *really* long day.

"Jasper is in Maddox's office. He mostly hides from the twins, but he might need to be let out. Have fun!" Chris waves to us.

"Bye!" Addie calls to Chris as she makes a beeline for the door, hurrying after Josie.

"Why's Jasper hiding?" The Dalmatian hasn't seemed scared of anything since they brought him home from the shelter.

Addie grins at the child she's holding. With blue eyes and pale hair, this one is a replica of Chris, while the one in my arms has Josie's coloring, with dark hair and eyes and tan skin. "I think he's scared of kids."

I eye the baby in my arms. Same, Jasper. Same.

The child in my arms—I mentally name him Thing One—has ratcheted up his volume. How can baby lungs make so much noise? Thing Two looks like he's preparing to add his voice to this symphony.

I hold Thing One at arm's length. "Well, what do we do with them?"

Addie looks at me. She's shifted Thing Two to her hip in what looks like a practiced move. "Play with them, feed them, change them. And then put them down for naps when they get cranky." Her lips quirk in an amused style. "Leo and James aren't too much for you, are they?"

I don't know if Leo is Thing One or Thing Two. And yes, clearly, I'm in way over my head. I should have started my childcare career with one baby. Or a cat, or a pet rock. After all, I couldn't even keep a plant alive.

"Nah, I'm good," I lie. "I'll just, uh..." I look around for something to appease Thing One's anger.

Addie giggles. "Here, let me take James."

She sets Thing Two—Leo, apparently—on the floor and plucks James out of my arms. The traitorous child immediately calms, his big brown eyes fixed on Addie's face.

Back off, kid. She's mine.

"Aren't you just too cute?" she coos. "You want to get down with your brother?"

"Are you allowed to just put them on the floor like that?"

She gives me a strange look. "Um, of course. How else would they learn to walk? Or crawl?"

I don't know. I figured it was something that just... happened. Like how baby birds fly when they get kicked out of the nest or something.

Movement in my peripheral vision catches my

attention. Leo has rolled onto all fours and has crawled over his brother, and is now making his way across the room—way faster than I figured a baby could go. Holy shit. "Do we..."

Addie follows my gaze. "Just keep an eye on him and kind of follow him around. If he goes for something he shouldn't have, redirect him."

She makes it sound so easy. I follow Leo—he seems like the easier option for some reason—and stay a few steps behind him while he explores. Okay, this isn't too bad. I just stay on top of him. Kids aren't so hard. I give Addie a triumphant smile. See? I could be a good dad.

The thought hits with a jolt. I've managed to put Ellie almost completely out of my mind until right now. For a second, I wish she could see me now, that I could prove to her that the past has nothing to do with who I am now.

"Don't let him eat that," Addie says, looking behind me.

I turn to find Leo with an electrical cord in his fat fist. He's easily ten feet away from where he was when I turned around for a second to look at Addie. Jesus.

"Put that down," I tell him.

Leo stares at me, nonplussed. He does not put the electrical cord down.

"Seriously, kid. Unhand the death wire."

He raises it toward his mouth.

"Hey! I said—"

Addie saunters past me. "No-no," she says to Leo, prying the cord out of his hand. She picks him up and sets him down several feet away and facing a different direction.

Leo crawls off that direction, presumably in search of something else lethal.

"You take James. He's calmer." Addie points to Thing One.

The only way I can remember who is who is their outfits, even though their features are so different from each other. Leo is in green, and James—aka Thing One —is in blue.

"Do you think their parents ever mixed them up when they were younger?" I ask. "Or did they always look different?"

James is sitting in the center of the room, a set of plastic blocks in front of him. There's no sign of the banshee that greeted me at the door. How do babies switch moods so fast?

Addie takes a dust bunny away from Leo, then turns him the opposite direction and lets him go. "Oh, yeah. Leo came out with black hair. Apparently that's how Chris was when she was born, too. His hair fell out when he was like two months old and grew in blond. But at first they had to paint a toenail to remember who was who."

"Not a bad idea. At least they're dressed differently."

The blocks sit abandoned in the center of the living room. I catch sight of a fat leg disappearing around the edge of the couch and follow it. No wonder Josie and Chris looked frazzled. You never get to sit down. How come the kids don't get tired? It's been less than twenty minutes and I'm ready for a break.

We spend the next hour following babies around the living room and removing items of varying lethality from their chubby little hands. I know everyone talks about the effort involved in keeping their offspring alive, but I never knew it was because ten-month-olds are on a constant suicide mission.

My plan for today had been to spend some quality time with Addie. Just her and me, relaxing. I figured you feed them, put them down, and then do it all again in three hours. So far, it seems like I might have had the wrong idea.

Leo crawls by my feet. I keep an eye on his path until something putrid hits my nose. "Oh god."

Addie looks up from where she's sitting next to James. "What?"

"Holy f—fudge. It smells like sh—poop."

She snorts. "First, you can swear. They don't know words. All they say is 'da,' which is really a useless word when you have two moms. It's not like they're going to say 'fuck' as their first word if you let one slip. And if they do, it's because they heard it from Chris. She swears more than I do."

"Okay. But the real issue here is that something smells like *shit*." I lower my voice on the last word. I'm pretty sure Addie knows what she's talking about, but just in case. I don't want to be responsible for potty-mouthed toddlers.

"He probably has a dirty diaper. I can change him." She starts to get up.

Okay, I'm out of my depth, but I'm not a pansy. I can handle this. Addie is probably rethinking my suitability as a parent and thus as a long-term partner. I need to show her I've got this. That I can carry my weight when it comes to kids and the two of us working together. And if this is what it takes, I can handle some baby shit in the name of true love.

"I've got it," I say. I pick up Leo, holding the tiny stink bomb as far away from my nose as possible.

"Okay." She doesn't look at all confident in my

ability to execute this. "The changing area is in the guest room. Right over there." She points, and I carry Leo that direction.

By the time I push open the door with my foot, Leo has made it abundantly clear that he does not want to be carried, does not want his diaper changed, and hates me with the fire of a thousand suns.

"Be cool, kid," I whisper as I lay him on the changing pad.

He rolls, almost launching himself off the table.

"Stay." I put a hand on his abdomen while I pull a new diaper and a pack of wipes off the shelf.

Okay. This is simple. Take the old diaper off, wipe, put the new one on. I unsnap his onesie and study the new diaper in relation to the old one. So the little yellow pieces go in the back and wrap around the front. Got it.

I set the clean diaper to the side and pull a wipe out. I'm ready for anything you've got, kid. The tabs peel off and I pull the diaper down to find a shitload of shit. One wipe isn't possibly going to do it.

It takes nine wipes—eight for the diaper area, one to clean Leo's hand—but the poop is contained, or at least in a pile out of his reach. I take one more wipe— may as well make it an even ten—and clean his butt once more. Perfect.

I add the wipe to the dirty pile and reach for the new diaper. Tuck it under, pull it up, and—

"Fuck!" I shriek, as Leo fires directly at me. I put my hand over the yellow stream. "Oh, fuck fuck fuck. You little fucker." Pee drips down my cheek. He almost hit my *mouth*.

Addie comes rushing in, Thing One under her arm like a sack of potatoes. "What happened? Is Leo alright?"

"The fucker peed on me!" I sputter.

Addie just stares for a minute. Her lips twitch, like she's trying to hold back a smile, but she loses that battle with a little snort that swiftly turns into full-on laughter. She puts James in the crib behind her, and when she straightens, she's laughing so hard there are tears in her eyes.

I stand there, baby urine dripping from my hand and my chin, while she tries to pull it together.

"Oh my God," she says, wiping her tears. "This is about the funniest thing I've ever seen. Josie is going to love this story."

"Don't you dare tell her!" That's all I need, a reputation as the guy who can't change babies without getting peed on. I've seen the way the Andersons gossip at holiday gatherings. This story has potential to become one that gets told over and over, and I'll never live it down. "And can you help me here?"

Addie is still laughing softly. "Go get cleaned up. And never leave the wee-wee uncovered." She grabs a new diaper, still holding the pee-soaked one in place.

As I slink off to the bathroom, it sounds like Leo is laughing at me, too.

I stick with James for the rest of the afternoon. He, at least, hasn't peed on me, and when he unleashes something in his diaper, I meekly hand him to Addie to be changed.

She takes him with a smirk on her face. "Don't let Leo eat dirt while I'm gone."

Leo does not eat dirt. Leo decides that this is the moment that we have all been waiting for to hear his new screech, which he demonstrates at top volume. And keeps demonstrating.

Addie rushes back into the living room, carrying James tucked under her arm like a football. "What happened? Is he okay?"

I gesture meekly toward the child in the center of the room. "He just... started. I don't know what triggered it. Is there an off switch?"

She hands James to me and disappears into the kitchen, coming back with two bottles just as James seems to be contemplating joining his brother's serenade. I'm going to invest in ear plugs before I babysit again.

Who am I kidding? I'm never babysitting again. A vasectomy is looking pretty good right now, honestly.

Addie hands one of the bottles to me. I angle it toward James, and he grips it with his chubby baby hands as I put the nipple in his mouth, then awkwardly try to balance him in my arms. Addie just sticks the other bottle in Leo's open mouth, then scoops up the whole bundle into her arms while Leo sucks contentedly on his bottle.

"They'll probably go down for a nap after they finish," she whispers. "Try to keep things quiet and calm."

Yeah, cause I'm the one who's been making this day anything less than *quiet and calm*.

Addie is right, of course. James's eyes get heavy as he reaches the end of the bottle. At one point I try to pull it out of his mouth, but he sucks it back in, so I let it stay there. Finally, it slips from his mouth as his breathing evens out.

I look up at Addie. "Now what?" I whisper.

"Follow me. Move slowly and smoothly." She

climbs to her feet with the grace of a ballerina, holding Leo steady, and I do my best to copy her. We tiptoe together toward the guest room where two cribs are set up. James stirs briefly, and I freeze, but he settles back into sleep.

"Now you slooooowwwly lower him down," Addie says, drawing the word out as she places Leo in the crib like she's handling an active bomb, "then back away, one step at a time. Don't look away. Don't show fear."

25

ADDISON

To: AAnderson@brynmawrschools.com
From: PSmith@brynmawrschools.com
Subject: Re: Senior class advisor

Hi Ms. Anderson,

Hope your break is going well. I have to admit your
lack of response has me a bit worried; I hope you're
safe and healthy. Can you give me a final answer on
your ability to commit to being senior class advisor? It
would mean a lot to the students.

Patricia Smith
Vice Principal, Bryn Mawr High School

T pull the door shut behind us, turning the knob before I close it so the click of the door latching won't wake the babies. I press my ear to the door after it's closed, waiting for any wails of distress, but it's silent, and I breathe a sigh of relief. *Finally*.

I stick my head into Maddox's office, coaxing out the Dalmatian that's doing its best to hide under the desk. "Come on, Jasper," I croon. "The babies are asleep. You can come out now."

I tilt my head toward the living room. Cam and Jasper follow me silently, and Cam and I both sink onto the large couch in the center of the room while Jasper settles at our feet with a huff, lowering his head to his paws.

"Holy fuck," Cam breathes, pushing a hand through his hair.

I'd laugh, but I'm feeling exactly the same. I'd forgotten how much work a baby is, let alone two. I used to help my mom with the little ones when she cared for foster kids, especially once Maddox and Josie were grown and out of the house.

"Yeah," I say, shaking my head. "They're a handful. I can't imagine having to be responsible for a kid all the time. An afternoon is plenty." I frown. "I mean, maybe someday. Not right now, at least. And maybe it's different when it's your kid."

Cam slides an arm around me and squeezes my shoulder. "You're going to be an amazing mom one day, Addie. Baby pee and all."

I look at him, trying to read his expression, but he looks completely sincere.

"Seriously," he insists.

I'm not sure how to answer that. I've always been terrible at receiving compliments. I settle for just twirling my hair around my finger while studying the baby monitor.

"Addie," he says, pulling away to look me fully in the eye. "Is that something you want? For real? Marriage, kids, a house, all of it?"

I'm not sure how to answer that. This has gotten so serious so fast. All of a sudden, too many emotions are rushing through me, and I don't know which ones to trust. I like Cam. More than like him, actually. So much that it scares me.

I want to tell him everything and to know everything about him. I've known him for so long, but it feels like I've barely scratched the surface of who he really is.

And I don't even know the right answer. Is there

one in this situation? If I say the wrong thing right now, are we going to be over?

I look down at my lap, away from his prying gaze, and shrug. "Someday, maybe."

He places two fingers below my chin and tips my face upward, so I have no choice but to meet his gaze. "It's not a quiz, Addie. I just—" He swallows, and I realize this is as hard for him as it is for me. "I just want to make sure we're on the same page. That we talk to each other. I want to be honest with you."

This might be digging too deep, but I need to ask. "What happened with your last girlfriend?"

Now it's Cam's turn to look away. He stares at the picture on the wall for so long that I start to wonder if there's more to it than a simple seascape, but finally, he swallows hard. "She cheated on me."

My heart squeezes, hurting for him. "I'm so sorry, Cam. That's so hard."

He shakes his head, still not looking at me. "There's more. It was a messy situation. It was while we were on a break, so I can't exactly expect her to stay loyal when we're not together. But it was complicated. I'm not ready to talk about all the details just yet, honestly."

He trails off. I'm itching to fill in the silence. I channel my social worker sister-in-law, queen of letting people sit with their silence, even though it's killing me to wait.

"That's why I was in such a bad mood at Holly and Maddox's wedding. Why I was so thrown to see you show up on the cruise instead of Maddox. I was ready to wallow in my pain, to do whatever I had to do to get her off my mind. I promised myself I wouldn't let myself fall for anyone for a long time. Maybe ever."

"I..." I'm not sure what to say. I'm not entirely sure what he's saying, what it means for us.

He shakes head. "I'm not done, Addie. I need you to hear this. When you showed up on the ship, I shouldn't have been such a dick. It was never about you. It was all my shit. All the times I pushed you away, it was because of my issues. But I care about you. I have for a long time, and this past week it's turned into more. At first, I thought I needed to keep you away from other guys in order to protect you. But it was to protect me. Because I don't want you with anyone but me."

It makes sense, now. The way he was so closed off, how he needed time. I'm not upset about him pushing away other guys; none of them were the ones I needed. It was always him.

"It's okay, Cam," I say, and I mean it. I want to kill Ellie for what she put him through, but at the same time thank her for letting him go so Cam and I had a chance.

We curl closer and closer together as we talk through the twin's naps. He tells me about his first love, a girl named Shannon from back in college. I feel a stab of jealousy when he tells me how they were one another's firsts, and I tell him about the college boyfriend that I lost my virginity to.

I tell him about the stress at work, about having to tutor to make ends meet, and how it's been almost two years since I've really dated anyone. How I stretch myself thin sometimes to make other people happy, thinking that seeing them content will make me happy, too.

When he asks if it works out that way, whether I'm really happy when I go out of my way to serve other people, I'm not sure I have an answer.

We talk more about Ellie—not all the details, and I don't push—but about the hold she had on him. How hard he tried to make it work, even down to babysitting a house plant that Ellie named Agatha. Which is a dumb name, if you ask me. I only admit that when Cam tells me that Ellie was the one who named it.

It seems like I'm getting to know a new side of Cam, and I wonder how much he shares with Maddox and his friends.

"Come here," he says, after I tell him about how I've grown up worrying that I'll never live up to Maddox and Josie, that the years between us made them idealized in my mind, and how far ahead of me they've always been with their lives. He pulls me close and brushes a kiss across my lips.

"Waahhh!" A shriek comes from the direction of the guest room, amplified by the baby monitor. We jump apart as the screech increases in volume.

"Shit. They're up," I say with a wince, standing and heading in that direction.

"Sounds like just one—" Cam breaks off as the second cry starts. I love his optimism that somehow one of them might sleep through the wail of the other.

I direct Cam as I lift James out of his crib and hand him to Cam, then pick up Leo. "Check his diaper, and then we'll get them something to eat."

"They just ate," he mutters, putting James on the changing table. He remembers to keep everything covered this time, which is progress, but the sight of Cam with baby pee dripping down his cheek will live forever in my memory.

I change Leo, and we carry the twins to the kitchen and strap them into their high chairs.

"This is... a lot," he says, putting the tray in front of Leo.

"Twins is definitely a lot."

He looks over his shoulder at me. "I want kids. Don't take that the wrong way. I think it'd be fun. But one at a time, preferably."

I nod as I cut up an avocado for the boys. "I think the chance of twins is pretty rare." Thank goodness. Because one baby is plenty of work.

"Isn't it a higher chance if there's twins in your family?" He looks so worried that I can't help but laugh.

"Josie did IVF. They put two of them in there in the first place. Plus, even if it was natural, I'm not actually related to Josie by blood." I love when people forget we're all adopted, though.

"Oh. Right." He breathes a sigh of relief, which is kind of adorable, and also kind of terrifying, because it means he's considering having kids. With me, if I'm reading things right, which is even more terrifying, but maybe not a bridge we need to cross just yet.

I set tiny pieces of avocado in front of each of the twins, one or two at a time. They grip each piece so tight it's a squished mess by the time they smear it on their faces.

"It looks like they ate Kermit the Frog," Cam comments, scrunching his nose.

I giggle. "Kind of. At least it's on their face and not

on the—" I break off and sigh as James throws his avocado off the tray. "Floor. I'll pick it up when they're done. Cleaning while they're still eating is like shoveling while it's still snowing. Pointless and you'll just get a bunch on your head."

I end up having to slice another avocado, because the twins just keep eating. And eating.

I suddenly remember the email my mother sent me about how many these boys eat. Didn't she say they went through like fourteen or fifteen in a few days?

"Maybe if you boys would eat fewer avocados, your moms could afford a house," I joke, even though Chris and Josie already own their home. Just outside of Boston, which is a little far away if you ask me, but they love it there.

We follow the twins around as they explore the non-baby-proofed house. Cam is definitely out of his depth, but I admire the way he's not only sticking with it, but also trying to maintain a good attitude. And if anything, he's gotten more comfortable over the last couple hours.

I know a lot of guys who would have said "*fuck this*" and left after the pee incident. Because if you want to get technical, this is *my* family. *My* sister asked me to babysit. These are *my* nephews. Cam is just along for the ride.

My heart warms as I watch him across the room, his eyes on Leo.

"Come here, you little terrorist," Cam says, darting toward the baby. He removes Leo's hand from where it's gripping Jasper's fur and sets the baby down in the opposite direction.

Jasper, for his part, looks tortured, but he continues to sit there dutifully while the twins use him as a jungle gym.

Cam detours toward James, who is reaching under the couch for something. I gag a little as he comes up with a dust bunny and sticks it in his mouth. Cam reaches for him, and I follow Leo to where he's trying to climb the stairs. It's only been a few hours, and we've settled into an easy rhythm.

I lift Leo into my arms and carry him back toward the living room. Cam looks over at me and smiles. He has James in his arms, the dust bunny now gone. I tilt my head and smile back as Cam walks toward me. Maybe he's getting the hang of this baby thing after all.

I shift Leo to my hip as Cam leans in and kisses me, slow and sweet. The babies actually respect our moment, both of them silent in our arms. I'm lost in the feel of Cam's lips on mine.

I don't even hear the front door open, until Josie speaks up.

"Um, hi. How's it going?" my sister asks.

Cam and I break apart to exchange wary glances. *Shit.*

We're going to have to tell Maddox before Josie does.

26

CAM

A loud knocking on my door makes me jump. I set down the soda can on the coffee table before I stand and open the door to find Maddox. I'm about to ask him how his honeymoon was when I see the expression on his face.

He's not here to chat. He's pissed.

"What the hell did you do to my sister?" he demands.

Shit. I was supposed to be the one to tell him. Did Addie say something? Did Josie rat us out?

If anything, my money is on Josie mentioning it in a benign way, probably blissfully unaware that she was supposed to keep this relationship under wraps.

"Come on in," I say as he barges past me.

Maddox stalks into the living room before he

whirls on me, pulling on the back of his neck. "So? Is it true?"

"Is what true?" I know exactly what he's talking about. I'm just trying to buy time here to work out a response that won't get Addie in trouble and won't give him any more ammunition to want to kill me.

"You're fucking my sister. I heard the whole thing from Josie. I got back from my honeymoon last night and this is what gets dropped on me. She left you with her kids and you were making out?" His glare is accusatory.

I shake my head. "I—"

"Don't fucking lie to me, Cam. Have a little more respect for our friendship."

I hold up my hand. "I'm not fucking her, man. I'm in love with her."

Time slows to a halt. I'm in love with her? The words came out of my mouth, but I hadn't really considered the possibility until just now. She's not just some girl I'm fucking. And she's not someone I'm casually dating, either. She's the woman I want to be with every minute of every day, and if I have my way, for years to come.

Is this what love is? I never felt anything like this with Ellie, or with anyone who came before her. It occurs to me that everything Ellie did to me sent me on a direct path into Addie's arms, maybe the one good thing that came out of my relationship with her.

"No." Maddox crosses his arms over his chest. "You're not in love with her. Don't fuck with me."

I nod slowly. "I only realized it myself just now. But it's real, Maddox."

A muscle in his jaw twitches. His eyes narrow. "How?"

I'm not sure I know, honestly. "I've known her for a long time."

"Since she was fucking *thirteen*!" he bellows, and I cringe as I see his point. She was a kid. I had no business looking at her that way back then.

But that was a long time ago, and we're both adults now. "Right. So a long time, since she's twenty-seven now. An adult." I arch my brow at him. "And when we were on that cruise, and in the Bahamas, we got to... know one another better. Realized how right we are together. And for the record, we weren't making out when we were watching the twins. I kissed her. Once."

"You told me you were going for a rebound on that cruise. Is that what she is to you?" He clenches a fist, then releases it.

The idea of Addie being anyone's rebound makes my stomach twist, and I understand his viewpoint. "No! I promise you, man. I'd never do that to Addie."

He gives a short nod. "Damn right you won't. So what happened? I've told you a million times to stay away from her. The age difference is one thing. But then you go and hook up with her while you're in this mindset? Maybe she's not a rebound to you now, but I don't get how I shouldn't be pissed at you for starting something in that frame of mind. Really, I don't. And I don't know why I shouldn't punch you in the face for this."

I get the feeling he's not in the mood for me to make a quip about how I want my face to look nice when Addie comes over later today. How can I get him to understand how deep this thing between us is?

I stand straighter. "Because she's not a little kid anymore, Maddox. She's an adult, and one I care about. And she deserves to make up her own mind."

He blows out a long breath and drops to the couch. "I want the best for her, Cam. You know I do."

"So do I," I say, but he's not listening.

Maddox rubs his hands over the knees of his jeans. "You're my best friend. I love you, man. And you know I want what's best for you, too."

I wait for him to come around to it. To say that it's great that two people he loves are in love with one another, even if it's just me that's at that point right now. To say he's happy for us. To apologize for barging in here like an asshole. That last one might be a stretch. But the rest of them.

But when he meets my eyes, his gaze is pleading, bordering on hard. I've seen this look before. He's placed his bets and he's going all in on what he thinks is right.

"Addie is family, though. And I have to put her first. She's younger than we are, Cam. She's in a different place than you are in your life. Don't pursue this. Please."

I sink onto the couch, most of the fight ebbing out of me. I never pictured Addie and me going this way. I knew Maddox would be upset, but I figured, optimistically, that once he heard that there were real feelings here, that this wasn't some fling or a one-time thing, he'd support it. That he wouldn't care about the age difference or how different Addie and I are.

After all, he's one to talk about pursuing someone who looks wrong for him on paper. And look how that turned out. He and his technically-stepsister are happily married.

I wonder what Holly has to say about this situation, come to think of it. She and Addie are practically best friends. They're the same age, so Maddox doesn't have a leg to stand on when it comes to the age gap between Addie and me, other than the timing of how we first met. Plus, I know Holly would set him straight if he was in the wrong.

I pull on the back of my neck, trying to think clearly. Maddox needs time to come around to this. From the muscle twitching in his jaw to his arms fixed across his chest, it's obvious he's not open to hearing my viewpoint here. So how do I choose between my best friend and the girl I think I'm in love with?

No, not think. I know. Maybe I don't have the balls to tell her just yet, and I'm not sure she feels the same way about me, but I'm ready to place my bets. I won't fold on this gamble.

I'm willing to give it time, to slow down. But under Maddox's glare, I'm starting to second guess everything. He's her brother, after all. Who am I to think I know what's best for Addie? I love her. But he's the one who's known her almost her whole life. Maybe there's something he knows that I don't.

Suddenly, everything I felt that day, back when Ellie dropped her bomb on me, pales in comparison to how I feel now. My heart didn't break with Ellie, not really.

But if I give up Addie, it's going to shatter.

"Walk away, Cam. Trust me. It's what's best," Maddox says, and all I can do is nod.

Because I'll do anything for Addie. Even walk away, if that's what she needs.

Everything inside me is cold and dark as I think of my life without her in it. She lights up a room, and I've already gotten used to her lighting up my life. I'll call her, see what else she has going on, see if there's a way we can make this work.

Together, as a team. And if there's something that we can't get past, at least I'll know what it is.

I'm going over this plan in my head when Maddox picks up my phone—my brand-new phone, the one I programmed Addie's number into first when I got it— from where it was sitting on the coffee table, next to my half-empty soda can, and holds it out to me. "Do it now."

27

ADDISON

To: AAnderson@brynmawrschools.com
From: PSmith@brynmawrschools.com
Subject: Re: Senior class advisor

Hi Ms. Anderson,

Thanks so much for agreeing to take this on. The students will be thrilled. Prom committee meets every Thursday after school until 3:30. The next meeting is this upcoming week after the students return from their spring break. I'll forward you the rest of the meeting schedule.

Patricia Smith
Vice Principal, Bryn Mawr High School

. . .

Agreeing to be the advisor for the senior class was a mistake of gargantuan proportions, as my dad used to say. I press my fingers to the spot between my eyes, trying to stave off the impending headache.

The prom committee, which I apparently now also advise as part of these duties, is split right down the middle. Half of them want a theme to prom, like an old-school Under the Sea or 1990s or something. The other half want no theme at all. They've been arguing this point for the last forty-three minutes. I should have listened to Annika and just said no. I wonder if there's a non-confrontational way out of this.

My phone buzzes in my pocket. I pull it out, just grateful to have something to focus on other than the adolescent squabbling.

CAM

I think we need to talk about what we're doing, see if it's the right thing to pursue this relationship. I promise I just want what's best for you.

What? My stomach bottoms out, and I reread the message as my hands start to shake. No. This isn't right, is it? Cam was more certain than I was about all of this. And now I get this message? It's not a breakup, but it's damn close.

My entire body starts to vibrate with anger, and I read the message again. Oh, he wants what's best for me, does he? And that's why he's questioning our relationship?

When I was younger, my family teased me so much about the *Hurricane Addie* thing that I tried everything to keep my temper under wraps, which was the reason for the hurricanes in the first place. Trying to hold my emotions in so I'd be pleasant, happy Addie all the time made it so that when things bubbled up, they exploded, all that pent-up frustration needing somewhere to go.

And maybe as an adult, I should be better at controlling my temper. But I'm *pissed*. This text is a complete 180 from the last time we were together. We were talking about being serious, about the future, all of that. I was holding back some of my real feelings, things I think it's too early to feel.

And now this. Adding anger to the mix of emotions I've been holding onto is bringing things to a point of no return. My fingers start to tingle where they're holding the phone.

Something happened to make him question things

like this. Cam didn't come up with this on his own. And I'm tired of people in my life thinking they know what's best for me. I may be the baby of the family, but I'm a goddamn adult. I know what I need. And what I want.

And I'm going to go get it.

I stand up so abruptly that the folding chair nearly falls over. "I need to cut this short, guys. Think of ways to compromise for our meeting next week." A couple of the students start to whine, and I cut them off with a look I know they've never seen from me, but they should probably familiarize themselves with. "If there's no compromise, there's no prom. Good luck."

The students fall silent as I leave the room, some of them already pulling out cell phones to call their parents for a ride home.

I'm once again grateful that I teach high school. The drama can be a bitch, but I can leave if I need to. I don't need to walk them to their parents' cars and buckle them in like the kindergarten teachers do.

By the time I reach my car, I'm fuming, and I think I have a good idea about who deserves this anger. Like I said, this wasn't Cam's idea. I'll bet anything.

Maddox's house is in Wynnewood, only a few minutes away from where we grew up in Ardmore, and less than fifteen minutes from the school. The drive only makes my anger grow. I pull into his driveway and throw the car into park.

"Maddox!" I yell, hitting the doorbell several times in a row.

The door cracks open. Holly stands there, looking confused. She must have just gotten home from work, since she's still in her khakis and a button-down shirt. "Hey, Addie. I just got home. What's—"

"Where is he?" I fume.

Holly takes a step back, opening the door wider to let me in. She knows exactly who I'm talking about. "He's in the office. Is everything okay?"

I stalk that direction without answering her. She lets me go, because she's seen Hurricane Addie, and she knows better than to get in the middle when the Anderson siblings fight. And I don't want to involve her.

She's always been firmly on Team Addie, but Team Addie and Team Maddox are usually aligned. I don't want to test her loyalty when I go head-to-head with her husband. I barge into the guest bedroom that Maddox uses as an office without knocking. He's seated at the desk playing online poker. Sorry, not sorry to interrupt your hard work, brother.

"What the hell did you say to Cam?" I yell.

Maddox spins around in his chair. He's seven years

older than me, and he's always been overprotective. I think in his mind, I stopped aging when he went off to college, and he still sees me as a preteen that needs her brother to watch out for her.

Usually, I don't mind. It's kind of sweet. But he's never overstepped this way before.

"Hi, Addie," he says, not answering the question.

"What did you say to him?" I demand again.

His eyebrow arches. "Why? Is there something going on between you two?" There's something in his expression, though. He knows there is. I'm just not sure he knows the extent of it. When Maddox gets something in his head, he doesn't stop until he gets what he's after. It was adorable when he was focused on Holly, but this is my life. Not his.

"Cut the shit, Maddox. You know we're together. I can see it written all over your face. We were going to tell you together, but you just couldn't wait, could you? Had to stick yourself in my business again?"

My voice is so loud I know Holly can hear, and I don't care. My sister-in-law is one of my best friends, and I'd bet anything she'd back me up on this.

He lets out a long sigh. "Addie, you know I love you."

Debatable right now, but I let him continue.

"Cam is my best friend. I've known him for a long time. He's not the right guy for you."

Now it's my turn to raise an eyebrow. "Out of curiosity, Maddox, just who *would* be the right guy for me? Some kid in middle school who just wants to hold my hand? Maybe take me to see a PG- rated movie? I'm twenty-seven, Maddox. I'm not a little kid you need to keep safe. This may come as a shock to you, but I've had sex before."

I can see his determination slip, and that's how I know I'm on the right track. This has nothing to do with Cam or any other guy. Maddox *knows* Cam is a good person. It's about me, and Maddox knows he's fighting a losing battle this time.

He blows out an agitated breath. "Addie, it's not that, and please don't ever talk to me again about having sex. I don't need to know those things. It's that Cam... he's got some things going on. He's not in a good spot for a relationship."

I lift my chin, meeting his gaze with my narrowed eyes as I cross my arms. He can try any angle he wants, but the end result is going to be the same. I'm not backing down this time. "The thing with Ellie? I know, Maddox. We talk. Cam and I aren't just fucking, although I'll have you know we're doing that too, and it's freaking amazing."

He looks supremely uncomfortable at this fact, which gives me great pleasure.

"The point is that this is real. It's not something you can insert yourself into in the name of some misguided protection or concern that I'm still a little kid. I know I've given you and the rest of the family the idea that I'll give in to anything you ask, because I'm a people pleaser. But I'm done bending over backwards and sacrificing what I want and what I need to make people happy. I deserve to be happy."

Maddox opens his mouth, but Hurricane Addie isn't done.

"And for the record, the only protection I need from Cam is a condom. Preferably a lot of them." Now I'm done. And particularly proud of that last comment, which has made Maddox's face turn a satisfying shade of purple.

A muscle in his jaw ticks. I know he's thinking through his response, deciding whether to give in to the hurricane or to stand his ground.

And I realize I don't actually care. I don't need his approval. I was serious. I'm done making decisions based on how it will affect other people. Maddox is my brother and I love him, but this thing with Cam is real.

"You know what, Maddox? I don't need to know what you said. Cam will tell me. And I don't need your approval. I'm doing this because it's what I want. I love you and I hope you can support me in this, and I hope you'll support Cam, because he loves you, too. Just... make good choices," I say, ending with the advice my mom loves to give.

Maddox sits there, stunned, as I whirl around and stomp through his house and back to my car.

Cam lives in the city, which is a colossal pain in the ass with parking in downtown Philadelphia. After circling the block twice I manage to find a pay-by-the-hour spot at a lot near his apartment and swing into a parking space.

It's not quite warm enough for the sewer smell to waft up from below ground. This would actually be a nice day for a walk in one of the city parks or by the river if I weren't so pissed off.

His apartment building is nice enough to have a doorman, who stops me as I stomp across the lobby.

"Who are you here to see?" he asks, all professional despite the fact that I'm clearly still fuming.

"Camden Allen. 9B," I answer.

He picks up a phone. "And who can I say is here to see him?"

"Oh, he'll know who it is." I cross my arms over my chest.

The doorman keeps his gaze on me. He looks vaguely afraid of me, and he should be. "Yes, Mr. Allen? I have a visitor for you. She... says you'll know who it is?" He nods, then hangs up the phone. "You may head up. And he says to... leave the hurricane in the lobby."

"Thanks," I say, ignoring his bewildered expression as I walk toward the elevator and punch the button.

Cam is waiting at his apartment door when I step off the elevator. He shifts from one foot to the other as I approach. "Addie," he starts, pulling at the back of his neck.

"I'm mad at you too, Cam. What the hell?" I toss my hands in the air.

He just opens his door to let me in, his shoulders slumped. I go to the living room and drop my purse on the couch. Cam follows me and plops onto a chair with a huff.

He pushes his hand through his hair, leaving it even more spiked and unruly. "I'm sorry, Addie."

"Seriously, Cam? That's all you have to say? I want the truth. What changed for you?" Now that I'm standing in front of Cam, the hurricane is dying a bit. I mean, not entirely.

We're still at tropical storm level, or maybe just thunderstorm. But Cam is a calming presence. It's hard to stay so mad when he's looking at me that way. I pause and pull in a deep breath. I just keep remembering the way he encouraged me to let everything out, and then held me when we were in Nassau.

"Get it all out," he says, and I know I'm so far gone when it comes to this man. "Let all the anger out, and then we'll talk."

I blow out a breath and look him in the eye. "Was it Maddox? Just tell me that much."

He nods, confirming what I already knew. The two of them talked about me behind my back. And knowing that two of the men I trust most in the world tried to make decisions for me, thought they knew better than I did, just reignites the flames.

I pace in front of Cam. "I don't know why you two assholes think you know best. I may be younger than you two, but I'm not a kid. I'm old enough to make my own choices, and I'm sure as shit old enough that I won't accept being broken up with over text message, or whatever the hell you were trying to do with that text."

I point at Cam, who shrinks back slightly.

"That's the fucking coward's way out, and you know it. And this is real, Cam. This thing between us.

Don't throw it away because Maddox has some weird need to treat me like his baby sister. You know this is real. I fucking fell in love with you, you asshole. The least you can do is respect me enough to talk to me before you break up with me over whatever my brother said."

Cam's gaze hasn't left my face as I've paced back and forth while delivering my speech, but now that I'm done, his jaw is slack. He's staring at me in shock, not anger.

Oh, shit. I said the thing about falling in love.

Cam stands up, ignoring the throw pillow that falls to the ground and is next to me in two steps. He pulls me into his arms, holding me tight. I'm stiff against him, waiting for him to say something. Anything.

I push back enough to look up to his face, trying to read the emotions written there. His eyes crinkle at the edges. A little smile plays at his lips, like he thinks this is funny or something. I'm about to tell him just how not funny this is, how serious I am about all of this, but then his face softens, and the words catch in my throat.

"I fucking love you too, my little hurricane," he says, and his mouth comes crashing down on mine.

28

ADDISON

This is nothing like our first time together. It's fiery, angry, passionate. Our mouths come together in a clash of lips and teeth and tongues. My hands grasp at his shirt, fisting the soft cotton as I try to pull him even closer to me, and his fingers tangle in my hair.

All of the emotion of today bubbles up into need, fanning the flames between us.

"Fuck. Addie," he says, breathless.

I sink my teeth into his neck, just hard enough to leave a mark, and he lets out a hiss.

"Come here." He wraps his arms around me and lifts me. I curl my legs around his waist and hang on to his neck while he carries me toward the bedroom, our tongues still joined.

He stops short of the bedroom door and presses my back against the wall. His hard cock presses into my groin as he kisses me, long and deep.

"Take your pants off," he groans as he lowers me to the ground.

I shed my underwear and jeans, and my sweater too, leaving them in a heap on the floor as he does the same. This time, when he picks me up, there's nothing between us except my thin tank top. It reminds me of what I wore to bed on the ship those nights when I lay there thinking of him, wishing my body was up against his just like this. His cock presses at my entrance.

I roll my hips, but he holds me steady. "You're so fucking gorgeous, Addie."

I moan as he moves in just an inch into me. "More, Cam. Fuck."

"Yeah? Like this?" he taunts, his voice deepening as he pushes in the slightest bit more. It's not enough, and he knows it.

I just groan, moving my hips as I try to take him deeper, but he's in control here.

"Or did you mean like"—he thrusts into me, driving home in one quick movement, gravity pulling me down onto him to take him deeper—"this?"

I suck in a gasp as he bottoms out inside me. My head drops back as far as it can against the wall, and my eyes roll back in my head as I see stars. I'm so full, and it's so fucking good. "Oh God, Cam."

He flexes his hips. My body heats into a ball of flames, and I just need more.

He holds my hips, moving me up and down on his cock. I'm completely at his mercy as he holds me in place. His firm grip keeps me from falling and has him utterly in control as he fucks me hard.

He pushes me to the brink of an orgasm before abruptly pulling out and setting my feet on the floor, my tank top sliding easily against the wall. His arms stay around me, holding me upright, because my legs don't work anymore.

He sweeps me up in bridal-style as he brings me into the bedroom and places me gently on the bed, like I'm a fragile flower or a delicate piece of glass that might break, completely at odds from the way he took me up against the wall. His eyes never leave my face.

Cam leans over me and pulls my tank top up and over my head, leaving me bare. A shiver runs through me, goosebumps rising on my arms.

He runs his hands down my sides, his thumbs skimming over my taut nipples. "So fucking gorgeous, Addie," he says again, his voice reverent. He nudges my legs apart, settling between them.

"I need you, Cam," I rasp. My voice is strained

with the need to feel him inside me, to be closer to him.

"There are things I need to tell you, Addie," he says, holding my gaze. His hand traces my jaw. "This is real. I want you to know everything."

I shake my head. "I want to know everything, too. But not now. Right now, I just want to feel you. I don't give a fuck about anything else. Nothing you can tell me is going to keep us apart."

Cam fists the base of his cock, directing it to my entrance. "You might change your mind once you know, Addie. But it's going to be your choice. No one else's. I'm not going anywhere. I'm yours. For however long you want me."

I open my mouth, ready to tell Cam again that nothing he could say will change my mind, that I want him for as long as I can have him too, but as he sheathes himself inside me in one long thrust, the only sound that comes out is a euphoric cry.

He fucks me slow and hard and deep, taking his time between thrusts that hammer me into the mattress below. An orgasm creeps up and overtakes me without warning, and as my pussy squeezes around him, he starts to move faster.

I cry out his name as stars cloud my vision. I've never come this hard with anyone, not ever. It's this overwhelming sensation that takes over my body completely, the waves of bliss washing over me. My muscles are so tight I can't get a breath in.

I can't tell how long I'm trapped in the throes of my climax, but when I finally pull in a breath and open my eyes, my entire body tingling, Cam is smiling down at me.

"Fuck," I say, breathless. "That was intense. *Good* intense."

"Yeah?" he murmurs, moving his hips, and that's when I realize he's still buried deep inside me. And he's still hard.

My eyes are wide as I look at him. I'm not sure I can do that again. Another orgasm like that just might kill me. I'd die a happy woman, though.

"How's your arm?" Cam asks, moving lazily in long, slow strokes.

"My what?" I blink at him.

"Your arm, Addie. Your stitches."

My body isn't my own right now. I look down at the shoulder Cam is brushing a finger over and realize the spot where I had the stitches is starting to scar. It's sensitive, but not really painful anymore. "Oh. Uh. It's okay, I think. Why?"

Cam lets out a little laugh. "Because I'm just getting started, baby."

Somehow, he maneuvers us without putting any pressure on my arm, and I find myself at the edge of the bed on my stomach. My feet hang off, and my belly is flat against the mattress, but I don't have to put any weight on my arm.

Cam stands behind me, nudging my legs apart to stand between them. "God, you have a hot ass, Addie."

I giggle, and he brings his hand down on my backside. The noise makes me jump, but it's not hard enough to hurt, and by the time I even register the spank, he's massaging my ass with both hands.

"I've wanted to take you like this since I saw you in the gym."

I look over my shoulder, puzzled. "Gym?"

Cam nods. His hands grip my hips as he positions himself and starts to slide into me.

"On the cruise ship. You were lifting weights in that outfit. God, I wanted to tear it off you so no other guys would look at you. And so I could do this." He punctuates his words with a hard thrust, his fingers caressing my skin.

A whine escapes from my throat. I grasp for purchase, my fingers fisting in the bedsheets.

"Don't you ever wear that outfit again, Addie," he says between hard, punishing strokes. "No one but me gets to enjoy this ass. Isn't that right?"

"God. Oh God." It's all I can get out as he drives into me over and over.

"Tell me you're mine, Addie. That all of you is mine." His voice is deeper than usual, his tone dark and demanding. It's a side of Cam that you'd never guess lurks beneath his normal easygoing self.

And I'm the one who gets to see it.

"Fuck!" I gasp. "I'm your, Cam. All fucking yours."

"Damn right, baby." He reaches a hand around me to find my clit. "Come for me, my girl." He presses on the bundle of nerves, and I shatter around him as he comes, deep inside me.

Cam gathers me into his arms while I try to catch my breath, my heartbeat hammering inside my chest.

"You're so fucking incredible, baby," he says, murmuring the words into my hair.

All I can do is press a cheek to his chest, unable to speak. I'm not sure there are words that would do justice to what just happened. Every fiber of my being is completely consumed by this man.

We stay like this, our breathing slowing as we hold onto one another. When I'm finally able to talk, I tilt my head up to look at him as best I can from this angle. Even without a full view of his face—mostly, just his chin is visible from this position—his smile is tender, but there's a hint of amusement as his finger traces my jawline.

"Did you go off on Maddox before you came here?" he asks.

I nod, my cheeks heating a little. "I kind of unleashed the hurricane on him, too. I didn't even give him a chance to talk. Not really, anyway. I, uh... I might have told him that we've been fucking. He kind of turned purple."

Cam chuckles. "While the hurricane is terrifying when it's directed at me, that might have been a good use of your temper. And Addie?" He looks down at me, his expression growing serious. "I'm proud of you."

I furrow my brow. "Why?"

"So many reasons. But right now, I'm proud of you for standing up for yourself. Taking what you want. Not putting yourself second to what everyone else needs. Doing what you need to do for yourself, even if other people don't agree."

As I think about it, I realize he's spot on. This is one of the first times in my life I've really stood up to

Maddox, gone against what he thinks is right. "Maybe I just needed something worth fighting for," I whisper.

"What matters is that you did it, Addie. And Maddox will be fine. Once he comes around, he's going to be proud of you, too." Cam brushes a piece of hair off my forehead and kisses the spot where it was.

"I love you," I whisper.

He shifts so I can see his whole face. "I love you, too, Addie," he says, but his smile fades. "But it's time you knew more about some things. And if you change your mind about me, I'll understand."

29

CAM

My stomach twists. I've known this talk was coming. Honestly, with the way Addie and I have been able to talk about anything and everything, you'd think we would have discussed it already, instead of me having to drop it on her like a bomb while she's in a post-orgasmic haze.

God, she's so fucking beautiful too. Her cheeks are flushed, and her honey-brown eyes are bright. Her hair is fanned out across the pillow. I could look at her like this forever.

Actually, this is exactly the reason I haven't wanted to bring it up. Why I changed the subject when she asked about it earlier. Because this Addie—the sweet goddess in front of me, looking at me with those big, trusting eyes—is going to be gone once she knows. She won't look at me the same. It's going to change every-thing, isn't it?

Addie shakes her head. "It doesn't matter, Cam. Whatever it is, we can figure it out."

I take a deep breath. I'm not as optimistic as she is. "There's not just one thing, though, Addie."

This stuns her into silence long enough for me to get up the courage to say it.

"I told you that Ellie and I broke up for good because she cheated on me, that she slept with someone else. And it *did* happen while we were broken up—you know, we were on again, off again for a long time." I let out a sigh. "I think that's what wrecked me the most."

"It's that I put so much effort into making it work. I was always taught that relationships are hard work, and you have to put in effort to keep things going. But with Ellie, I was always the one doing all the work."

Addie nods, but she lets me keep going.

"The thing that really ended me and Ellie wasn't just that she slept with someone else. It's that she got pregnant with that guy's kid."

And there it is. The sharp intake of breath. I keep my gaze on my hands while I wait for Addie to point out how stupid I was to keep going back to her, how my judgment must have been so far off that I was willing to work on a relationship Ellie was so easily willing to throw away. I can't look her in the eye.

But instead, Addie lets her breath out in a sigh that mirrors mine. "That sucks, Cam. I can only imagine how that made you feel. To put in all the effort and have it turn out this way."

I raise my gaze to her face, searching for the disgust or the scorn that I expected, but there's only concern. Her features are soft, her eyes on me.

I nod, swallowing the lump in my throat. "Yeah. That's exactly what I was feeling. All that effort for nothing. And I didn't want to start a new relationship because I knew I didn't have the bandwidth to put in effort anymore. It wouldn't be fair to the person I was dating." I study her face for clues, but all I see is support. "But with you—it's easy, somehow. That's what pulled me in."

"So is that what Maddox was talking about? That Ellie got pregnant, that you weren't up for another relationship because of the effort it took?" Addie's eyebrows pull together in confusion. "I told him I knew everything, the whole story, because I trust you. I knew you'd tell me what I need to know. But is there something else?"

I swallow hard. "Maddox doesn't know Ellie got pregnant, actually. Just that we broke up and it's over for good. It was embarrassing, I guess, the idea that the girl I'd dated on and off for over two years could do that to me."

Addie tilts her head. "I get that. I really do, Cam. I'd never do something like that to you. And I understand if you need some time to get over it." She stretches up to plant a kiss on my lips.

I slide my hand behind her head and pull her closer, taking the kiss deeper. This might be my last chance to kiss her, depending on how she reacts to the next piece of information I have to share, and I want to make sure it's a good one.

Addie rubs a hand over her lips when she pulls back. "So what else is there, Cam? What's Maddox so weird about?"

I push a hand through my hair, my stomach sinking as I imagine how she's going to take this. "I'm not sure if this is really what's on Maddox's mind, to be fair. But it's on mine." I look her in the eye. "Back in college, one night, Maddox and I went out to a bar, and I drove us home at the end of the night. I'd had too much to drink, and I ended up getting in a car accident."

Addie's eyes widen. "Were you okay? Was anyone hurt?"

"No one was too badly hurt, thank goodness.

Maddox was okay. The other car had a lot of damage, but the driver was fine. I hit my head and had to get stitches. I got a DUI and had to do community service. It fucked up my scholarship, so I had to take out loans to finish school. And I have a record that will never go away."

My stomach twists, thinking of it. Remembering how disappointed my parents were, how they practically wrote me out of their lives after it happened. A card on my birthday every year is all the contact we have these days. It's why I spent almost every Christmas and Thanksgiving with the Andersons during college, and sometimes in the years after.

I force myself to meet Addie's gaze, even though I'm not ready to see the disappointment on her face, too. But her expression hasn't changed.

She fingers the scar above my eyebrow. "Is that where you got this?"

I nod. It's faded over the years, but it'll never go away completely.

Addie looks like she's thinking. Her brow wrinkles. "So... what does that have to do with dating me? It was forever ago." Then something shifts in her expression. "Wait, is *that* why you don't drink? Oh God, Cam. I'm so sorry. I shouldn't have been drinking in front of you. I had no idea. Shit. I wouldn't have done that if I'd known."

I just stare at her. She thinks *she's* the one in the wrong here?

"Addie, no. You can do whatever you want, I don't mind. And yes, it's why I don't drink, but I don't mind when other people do. It's more a combination of that and the fact that my dad was an alcoholic. He hasn't had a drink since I was really little, but he's always been open about it with us, so he was super upset when he found out about all of this. I think that's why they took it so badly."

Addie puts her arms around me. "Cam, I don't care what you did when you were in college. You were a different person. I was, too. Everyone makes mistakes when they're young. What matters is how you move on from them."

She still isn't getting it. My voice catches in my throat as I say, "Ellie said... she said that was why she was having a baby with another guy. Maybe it was an accident, but she said that with my past she didn't trust me to be the father her kid needed. And I know it wasn't fair to start something with you without telling you everything. I know you're going to see me differently now. I was hoping it wouldn't have to come up, but..."

Addie pulls away from me, just like I knew she would.

Like my parents did after the DUI.

Like Ellie.

But Addie is still looking right at me. "What the actual *fuck*, Cam?"

I blink. Once, twice. "I, uh…"

The hurricane is back, and now it's directed squarely at me for the second time today. Addie's eyes are less of a sweet honey-brown now and more like twin flames staring at me. "How *dare* you lump me in with her? And how dare you write *us* off like that, just because of something stupid she said? Who knows if she even meant it?"

"She did," I insist, but Addie's already firing up again.

"You have no way of knowing that. Even if she did, it has *nothing* to do with me. I get that she did a number on you, and you thought you had more time to get over it before you started something new. And if you need me to, I can back off until you're ready."

"But I'm not leaving, Cam. And I'm pissed that you would think I'd end the best thing I've ever had because of some stupid thing you did over ten years ago."

I'm stunned into silence.

"And Jesus, Cam. Stop punishing yourself for something you did back before you had a fully formed frontal lobe. Kids make mistakes. And you were a kid. You don't have to let it ruin your life. If you don't want to drink, don't drink. It shouldn't matter to anyone. It sure as shit doesn't matter to me. But don't use it as a way to tether yourself to the past."

I can't take my eyes off of her. Her hair is a tangled mess, and her makeup is smudged below her eyes. She's clutching the sheet to her chest with one hand while she uses the other to gesture dramatically to make her point. She looks absolutely nuts.

And fuck, I've never seen anything more gorgeous.

Her phone rings again from the floor, where it's in her jeans pocket. She ignored it the first two times, but now her gaze darts that direction. "Crap. If they're calling three times, it might be important. Let me get that."

She pulls the sheet with her while she retrieves the phone and puts it on speaker. "Hello?"

I just lean back on the pillow, content to watch her. I could spend the rest of my life watching her and be the happiest man in the world.

A woman's voice emanates from the speaker. "Miss Anderson. Am I understanding correctly that you walked out of the prom committee meeting?"

"Uh, yes, I did leave the meeting abruptly," she says.

I can almost hear the lady frown through the phone. "Miss Anderson, that's very unprofessional. It's not like you to walk away from your responsibilities."

Addie looks at me with a small smile on her face. "You know, Patricia, I've considered this some more, and I'm not able to take this on. Thank you for thinking of me, though."

There's a momentary silence. I don't think Addie has ever said no like this. It's a big step.

"We really need someone, Addison. Are you sure you can't help us with this?"

"Unfortunately, my answer is no. I'll see you tomorrow." Addie ends the call and lets out a long breath.

"You okay?" I ask.

She nods after a moment. "That was my vice principal. She asked me to be the senior class advisor and I originally said yes, because you know I can't say no when someone needs something. And then this afternoon when I got your text, I left in the middle of the meeting." She cringes. "I never do stuff like that. Never."

"But I've been thinking about how I go out of my way to make people happy, and how maybe I shouldn't all the time. Maybe it's time to prioritize me and my needs."

"Come here." I hold my arm out so she can snuggle in next to me. "I'm super proud of you. Holding your ground with Maddox was one thing. But with your boss? I'm impressed."

Addie runs her fingers over my chest. "Just... when it's something important, you have to go for it. Right?"

I stroke her hair. "Exactly. When you find something you want, you don't step away from the table. You place your bets and let it ride."

EPILOGUE
CAM, TWO MONTHS LATER

Miller shifts from foot to foot, running a finger around the collar of his button-down shirt. "Why did we have to do this? I look ridiculous."

I elbow him. "You look fine. We're doing this for Addie. So shut up and go supervise some teenagers or something."

Addie put her foot down on advising the prom committee, but she signed up to chaperone prom. Then, somehow, we were all agreeing to help out, and before any of us realized what we'd signed up for, we were pulling out suits to wear for the night. Blake, of course, got a free pass out of it because of something at the university. The rest of us are lined up against the wall of the high school cafeteria, which has been cleared of the usual tables and chairs and decorated with crepe paper in greens and blues.

Miller fidgets again. "I don't know anything about kids, let alone teenagers. Aren't they old enough to be on their own?"

Holly snorts, while Addie stares at Miller.

"Uh, teenagers aren't exactly self-sufficient. Or trustworthy," Addie says. "Some of them can make good decisions when they're alone or in a small group, but put them together like this and the bad ideas just multiply. Don't you remember being a teenager?"

"He's still waiting for his own frontal lobe to mature," I chuckle.

Miller elbows me.

Maddox walks toward us, escorting two boys who have guilty looks on their faces. One of them has something on his upper lip that looks like dirt. Is he trying to grow a mustache?

"What do you want me to do with these two?" he asks Addie. "They were outside smoking."

Addie rolls her eyes with a sigh. "Josiah, Ethan, you two know better. Give me the cigarettes."

The one with the failed attempt at facial hair shuffles his feet. "Uh, it wasn't cigarettes."

"Are you fu—" Addie catches herself. "Did you

bring marijuana in here, Josiah? I swear to God, what's wrong with you?"

"I'll hold onto it for them," Miller offers innocently.

Sure, he will.

"That shit's illegal, you guys," I add.

Addie glares at me. What? I was trying to help.

"It's not weed. Promise. It's just a vape," Ethan says earnestly. "Swear to God. Really. Please don't kick us out."

"Please, Miss Anderson? Ethan really wants to talk to Joanna Bloom," Josiah insists.

Addie looks like she's counting in her head. Finally, she says, "Okay. Hand over the vape. And one more toe out of line, you're both out of here and I'm calling your parents."

Josiah hands it to Addie, and the two of them scurry off.

"Maddox, follow them," she sighs, gesturing. "I don't trust either one of them."

He does, wandering across the dance floor a few feet behind the troublemakers as Addie hands the vape to me.

"Put this in your pocket. They don't get it back. We'll toss it at the end of the night."

I tuck it into my suit jacket pocket as the music

switches to a slow song. God, I hated this part of dances in high school. It's all fun and games until you have to find a girl to dance with.

Addie's gaze is fixed on something across the cafeteria. "Aw, look. He's asking her to dance."

I follow her gaze and see Ethan, sans vape, talking to a pretty girl with dark hair. "Is that the girl?"

Addie nods. "That's Joanna. She's way out of his league, if you ask me, but maybe she'll throw him a bone."

As we watch, Joanna hesitantly takes Ethan's hand, and the two move onto the dance floor. Addie sighs with contentment.

Another kid wanders toward us. He must be a football player with the thickness of his neck. How do they all end up with that? Is it something they focus on in the weight room?

"Hi, Rudy," Addie says. "Are you having fun?"

He shuffles. "Uh, yeah. I wanted to let you know that I got my SAT scores back. I got a 500 in math."

Addie's face breaks into a huge smile. "Rudy, that's great! I'm so proud of you."

Rudy smiles shyly. "Yeah. I think it'll be enough to get into a college I can play football at. Thanks, Miss A."

He wanders away, but the smile stays on Addie's

face. As proud as she is of that kid, I'm even more proud of her. Because she saw his potential and helped him get to this point.

"You want some?" Miller says, holding something out to Holly. Is that a flask? Leave it to Miller to embrace the full spirit of prom as though he were still an underage high schooler.

Holly visibly recoils. "No! I'm pregnant."

Addie's mouth falls open. "You're pregnant?" She glances at Miller with disdain. "I'll deal with you in a minute."

The two girls fall together, their faces lighting up with smiles.

"When did you find out? How far along are you?"

Holly's face is flushed. "Just a few weeks ago. I'm only nine weeks. I wasn't going to tell anyone yet, but it kind of slipped out."

Yeah, it wouldn't be the first time one of Miller's harebrained ideas pushed people a little too far.

Addie's smile mirrors Holly's. "I'm so excited! I can't wait to be an aunt. We have to plan a baby shower."

Maddox walks back up to the group, all of us doing a piss-poor job at actually supervising the teenagers.

"Congrats, daddy," Miller says, holding out the flask.

Maddox's eyes widen. He looks from Miller to Holly, and his expression softens. "Couldn't keep it in, could you?"

She shrugs, but it doesn't dim her smile.

"I'm glad you caved. It was torture keeping it from these guys." He takes a swig from the flask, then raises a brow. "Is this apple juice?"

Miller snatches the flask back and sips from it with all the air of a gentleman. "Yeah. Who the hell would bring booze to a high school prom? I figured it might be fun to give it to one of the kids and see if they thought they were drunk. Gotta amuse myself somehow, right?"

Yeah, that sounds about right. Miller's known for his pranks, but he's generally a good guy, and the pranks are mostly harmless.

Addie snatches the flask out of his hands with a groan. "Dear lord. It's more work to supervise you than the kids." She holds her hand out. "Give me the vape, too. I'm going to go put all of this in the car. Anyone else have any contraband they want to add to this pile?"

Miller hands over a pack of candy cigarettes. Addie rolls her eyes. "Don't do anything stupid while I'm gone. Holly, want to come with me? I need some girl time."

Addie and Holly disappear through the gym doors, leaving me, Maddox and Miller in charge, the blind leading the blind.

Miller leans against the wall. "Man. Spoil all my fun." He lets out a sigh. "I think I'm in a rut, you guys. I think I need a change."

"You could get married," I say. "Look at Maddox. He seems happy."

Maddox laughs. "Who's Miller going to marry? Plus, I have a feeling someone else is going to be the next one down the aisle."

A glimmer of something rises in me as he makes eye contact. "Is that your way of saying I have your permission?"

I asked Maddox a few days ago for permission to marry his sister. Obviously, Addie is the only one whose opinion really matters here, but somehow, I needed to know that I had my best friend's blessing.

He grins. "Only if she says yes. But you're already like my brother, man. This will just make it official."

Miller pushes off the wall as Maddox and I embrace. "You happy families make me sick. I need a change of scenery or something." He mock-scowls.

Maddox turns to look at him. "Well, Cam went on

spring break. Maybe you can do something over summer vacation. It's like you guys haven't matured past college."

Miller snorts. "You say that like it's a bad thing."

Holly and Addie walk back into the gym just as one song ends and another slow one starts. I can't take my eyes off Addie, her red hair brilliant against the green satin of her dress. I walk toward her, meeting her in the middle of the room.

"Hey," she says, that smile lighting her face.

I reach out and take her hand. "May I have this dance?"

Addie nods, and I pull her into me.

"Oooh, Miss Anderson's in loooove!" someone sing-songs. Freaking teenagers.

Addie looks me in the eye, her honey-brown irises sparkling. "They're not wrong."

"Love you too, Miss Anderson," I whisper, holding her close while we sway to the music.

"You know what's funny?" she murmurs, her head on my shoulder. "This is what I dreamed about back then, at my own high school prom. Dancing with you."

I pull back just enough to look her in the eye. "That's what I'm here for now, then. I want to spend the rest of my life making all of your dreams come true."

* * *

Miller's story is up next
in Betting on Love Book 3!

<u>Calling Your Bluff</u> is coming May 2024.
Preorder Now!

One easygoing poker player, one no-nonsense camp counselor, and two hidden pasts...

Why did I think I could become a camp counselor? As a professional poker player, my experience with kids is... limited, at best. What I thought would be a few days of fun by the lake is more intense than I ever could have imagined, and meeting my co-counselor was like a gut punch. She's smart and beautiful with biting wit and a smile for everyone—except me.

I don't know what I've done to make her hate me, and every attempt to win her over seems to backfire. Most people would fold—but I can't walk away from her, or from the sadness hiding behind her eyes.

She's determined to keep her secrets to herself, but she's not the only one hiding things. So when a camper is in danger, can we put aside our hidden pasts and work together? Or will our secrets cost us more than just our shot at love?

Fans of Meghan Quinn and Pippa Grant will love this steamy, reverse grumpy-sunshine romantic comedy.

ABOUT THE AUTHOR

Kate writes spicy contemporary romance and romantic comedy with all the feels. When she's not writing, you can find her cozying up to horses and telling her kids to clean their rooms while studiously avoiding cleaning her own space. She loves a good alpha hero and a happily ever after and thinks the best books should make you cry, at least a little.

She recently discovered the life-changing magic of cold brew coffee and believes ketchup is a food group unto itself.

Follow Kate on social media and sign up for her newsletter to be the first to know about new releases and freebies, and to hear Ollie the German Shepherd's life advice and book reviews.

(Disclaimer: Ollie is a dog. His advice is bad. Kate does not recommend following his advice. Unless you are a dog.)

Made in the USA
Middletown, DE
07 February 2024

48687503R00220